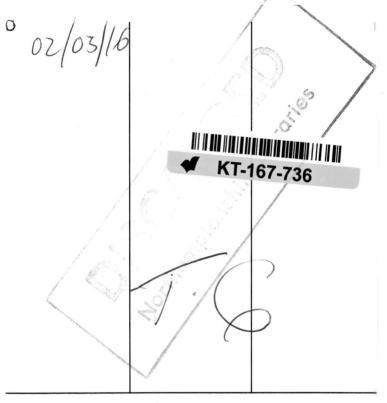

High Shoulders

Young drifter Tim Jackson is riding through the high country in search of fresh supplies and a job. As Jackson readies his faithful mount for a new day, he becomes aware they are not alone in the dense woodland. Shots begin to rain down on him just as he catches a glimpse of someone high above in the undergrowth. Jackson must summon every scrap of skill as a horseman and steer his grey stallion between the labyrinths of trees to escape the bullets.

As the mount comes to a halt at the edge of the forest, Jackson notices a town ahead. Hoping to find work, and believing he has outrun the ambusher, Jackson rides in. Accepting the job of sheriff quickly makes him enemies and soon there are bullets coming at him from every direction.

High Shoulders

Dale Mike Rogers

A Black Horse Western

ROBERT HALE · LONDON

© Dale Mike Rogers 2015
First published in Great Britain 2015

ISBN 978-0-7198-1801-1

Robert Hale Limited
Clerkenwell House
Clerkenwell Green
London EC1R 0HT

www.halebooks.com

Printed and bound in Great Britain by
CPI Antony Rowe, Chippenham and Eastbourne

Dedicated to Ocean Sue and Joshua

CHAPTER ONE

Tim Jackson kicked sand over the embers of his campfire and then rose to his full impressive height. Jackson rolled up his bed blanket and then turned to his horse. The grey stallion was like its master. It was tall. Really tall.

Jackson walked the ten feet to his mount and then placed the bedroll behind the saddle cantle and secured it with leather laces. The high-shouldered drifter glanced around the brush which surrounded him as his fingers worked.

Jackson tugged at his reins and then rested his hand on the saddle horn as his blue eyes surveyed the tree-covered hillside. A strange foreboding had haunted the six-and-a-half-foot tall youngster for more than a week now. It had become an eerie companion.

One which he had grown used to.

For some unexplained reason Jackson sensed that he was being trailed and yet no matter how hard he tried, he could not find any sign of anyone. His logical mind told him that it was his imagination and yet his heart kept warning him to be careful.

He might have only just reached his twenty-fifth birthday but he had already seen more than a dozen men killed. Some had died whilst labouring but a few had been cut down by the bullets of merciless killers.

Jackson had become very aware that the further west you roamed, the more likely you were to run up against well-notched guns. The young drifter knew that he was a high-shouldered target in these untamed parts.

He lifted his left leg and stepped into his stirrup. In one fluid action, he rose off the ground and swung his other long leg over the ornate saddle.

Jackson poked his right boot into the awaiting stirrup and then gathered in his long leathers. The sun was still low but rising gradually into the heavens. Its light filtered through the white barked trees, casting a mottled pattern across his temporary campsite.

He tugged at the leathers and turned the tall stallion until its nose was aiming downhill. His eyes sought and found a route down to the lush range below the hillside.

The grey obeyed his blunt spurs and started away from the still smoking embers. Jackson looked up and stared at the trail before him.

Yet the hairs on the nape of his neck tingled.

The drifter tilted his head and glanced over his wide shoulder. Once again he sensed that someone was watching his every move.

He tapped his spurs and the well-rested grey began to canter between the trees down into the depths of the unseen valley.

Jackson was correct.

Since he had entered the unfamiliar territory he had been observed and followed. Far up on the slope behind a massive boulder Rex Carter lowered his binoculars from his eyes and turned toward his own mount. He stuffed the glasses into one of the satchels of his saddlebags and then pulled his reins free of a nearby tree and swiftly threw himself up on to the back of his quarter horse.

Carter jerked the long leathers and started down after the high-shouldered cowboy. He withdrew his long rifle from its scabbard and lay it across his lap as his horse gathered pace.

His hand slid into the hand-guard.

His finger curled around its trigger.

Carter used every scrap of brush to conceal himself from the cowboy he doggedly pursued.

After less than five minutes riding in pursuit of the stranger, Carter knew that now was his chance. He pulled back on his reins, stopped his horse and then lifted the Winchester to his shoulder.

As Jackson cleared the trees and began to cross a small clearing, Carter squeezed his trigger. The shot echoed around the trees as its deadly lead hurtled through the air.

The bullet missed its large target by only inches. Yet Jackson felt the heat of the bullet. The drifter swiftly turned his mount and galloped back to the protection of the trees. He had only just reached a patch of sturdy saplings when another rifle shot rang out.

A million splinters cascaded over the horseman as he steadied his tall, grey stallion. The horse snorted as its master held it in check and drew one of his holstered six-shooters. He cocked its hammer and blasted a bullet back up the hillside in reply.

Jackson narrowed his eyes and caught a faint

glimpse of Carter as the gunman steered his mount back into the dense undergrowth.

Suddenly without warning a pair of rifle shots came hurtling through the trees and brush at him. The high-shouldered young horseman flinched as the bullets ripped into the trunk of a tree beside him.

Debris showered over both horse and rider.

Jackson fanned his gun hammer and blasted his gun three times in quick succession. He could hear the distressed sound of his attacker's horse as his bullets tore through the undergrowth.

He did not wait to discover whether his fevered shots had found their target. He pulled on his leathers, swung the grey around and spurred hard. Dust rose up behind the hoofs of the stallion as the stranger put distance between himself and the unseen Carter.

Carter felt the heat of Jackson's bullets as he ducked and his horse stumbled beneath him. His rifle fell to the ground as Carter wrestled with his long leathers. By the time the gunman had regained control of his mount, he knew that his chosen target had eluded him.

'Damn it all,' he cursed. 'I knew I should have plugged that *hombre* when I first seen him.'

Carter dismounted and snatched his Winchester back up. His eyes narrowed as he glared down at the distant hoof dust. He thrust the rifle into its saddle scabbard and fumed.

'Reckon I'd best go and explain how that *hombre* managed to get past me.' He snorted as he poked his boot toe into his stirrup and mounted again. He tapped his spurs and started to descend the tree covered hillside.

Unlike Jackson, he knew where he was heading.

CHAPTER TWO

The distant rooftops of a town could be seen catching the sunlight as Jackson navigated down through the trees toward it. He leaned back and caught the unmistakeable scent of chimney smoke drifting through the tree-covered hillside. The cowboy held his reins tightly and then narrowed his eyes. A score of wood-fuelled stoves were dispatching black smoke up into the blue sky. The aroma grew stronger the closer Jackson rode his sure-footed stallion toward the town.

Jackson ran a gloved hand across his dry mouth.

He was thirsty. The last drop of liquid to wet his lips and soothe his throat had been just after sundown the night before when he had finished the last of his coffee.

He pulled the head of the stallion toward him and stopped the animal from continuing down toward the town. He allowed the dust to pass his mount's long legs before looking around his resting-spot.

Jackson glanced over his broad shoulders in search of the precious liquid he craved. Yet the tree-covered hillside was as parched as he was.

If there was water somewhere on the hillside, he could not locate it. The ground was tinder dry and dusty between the trees. Jackson shook his head and was about to return his attention to the scattering of buildings he observed from his high vantage point when a sound behind him filled the air and alerted his keen senses.

A horse's hoof had just stepped upon a bone-dry twig. The silent woods had allowed the noise to carry to where he sat astride his grey.

Jackson twisted on his saddle and squinted up the steep slope he had only just travelled down. He focused hard to where he was sure the noise had come from. Dust floated on the air away from the dense undergrowth.

'So, there *is* someone trailing me,' he muttered.

He wondered who was following him and why. It gnawed at his craw. Jackson gave out a yell, slapped the rump of the grey and rode on down towards the town.

He knew that his wide shoulders made a mighty easy target for anyone with killing on their mind.

The skilful cowboy expertly steered a route between the trees as the grey stallion obeyed its master's commands. As the horse gathered pace, Jackson balanced in his stirrups and continued to look back through his mount's dust. No matter how hard the cowboy tried, his search was in vain. Rex Carter was like a bad smell that was impossible to see, but the cowboy instinctively knew he was there.

Jackson lashed the tail of his horse. The grey leapt over a fallen tree trunk. Its hoofs skidded on the loose ground and the animal nearly stumbled. Its fearless master yanked the reins back and steadied the grey as it strode down the last of the incline.

The ground levelled out. Jackson had cleared the trees and turned the grey to face the outskirts of the settlement. The scent of abundant water in troughs drew the horse beneath him like a fish to a baited hook.

Jackson did not pause for a solitary moment. His muscular arms cracked the long leathers and urged the grey on. As the stallion trotted into the unmarked boundaries of the settlement, Jackson looked all around him. The town was no more comforting than the trail which had led him to it.

Jackson felt anxious. It was early and there seemed to be no one on the boardwalks as he entered the main thoroughfare. It was like entering a ghost town.

He slowed the horse's advance as his eyes darted around the array of store-fronts and houses. The only thing which gave him some comfort was that a wooden shingle hung on a chain from a porch overhang. The words read: 'SHERIFF'.

Beads of sweat trailed down from the hatband of his battered Stetson. It had nothing to do with the blazing sun which beat down upon the settlement.

Jackson turned the grey and allowed it to walk toward the well-nourished water trough just outside the sheriff's office.

He drew rein as the horse lowered its head and started to drink. Still thoughtful of the fact that someone was trailing him, the cowboy looped his leg over his bedroll and dismounted. He tied the reins firmly to one of the uprights and plucked his rifle off the saddle.

He cranked its mechanism and gritted his teeth as he stared over his saddle at the road behind him. The road he had only just travelled along.

'Where is he?' he muttered to himself.

Yet no matter how hard he stared, there was no sign of anyone trailing him. Jackson lowered his Winchester and bit his lip thoughtfully.

He began to doubt himself.

The cowboy was convinced that he had been followed through the dense wooded hills yet there was not even the hint of a rider entering the town in his wake.

'You look kinda troubled, stranger.' A voice piped up from behind his wide shoulders.

Jackson turned and squinted. The sun dazzled his eyes as it reflected off the glass panes of the office. Finally, he saw a mature figure sporting a well-tailored suit and velvet top hat. The man seemed out of place in this town, Jackson thought as he stepped away from his horse and mounted the boardwalk.

'I *am* a tad troubled,' he responded with a touch of his Stetson brim. 'You see, I could have sworn that some *hombre* was following me.'

Jefferson Healy was nearly sixty and well rounded. He removed a long Havana from his lips and smiled as he tapped its ash free. His baggy eyes sparkled as he advanced toward the tall cowboy. He studied Jackson in a fashion most men reserved for horse-buying.

'Hell!' He sighed dramatically before leaning back and looking up into the face of the cowboy. 'They sure make them big where you come from, son!'

A smile traced across the face of the cowboy. He pushed the brim of his hat back until it rested on the back of his thick head of hair.

'They sure do,' he agreed.

'My name's Healy. Jefferson Healy,' the older man informed. 'I'm the mayor and I kinda run things in Broken Lance.'

'My name's Tim Jackson.' Jackson raised his eyebrows and looked at the street. 'So this is Broken Lance? I wondered where in tarnation I was.'

'Where were you headed?' Healy enquired.

'Any place that might have a job for a large man with a tall horse to feed, Mr Healy,' Jackson said honestly. 'Has Broken Lance got any jobs it wants to fill?'

Healy sucked on his cigar and walked slowly around the tall cowboy. Once again it appeared that he was studying horse flesh and not another man.

'It so happens we *do* have a job that might suit

you.' Healy nodded.

Jackson sighed as the heat of the rising sun started to drain the sap from his enormous frame. He dried his temple with the tails of his bandana and looked down upon the prosperous-looking man.

'What kinda job is it?' he asked. 'I'm not too fussy when my belly is as empty as my billfold.'

Healy removed the cigar from his lips and tapped the ash carefully onto the ground. His eyes glanced at the cowboy and a smile favoured the corners of his mouth.

'Lawman,' he answered before pointing the Havana at the sheriff's office beside them. 'Sheriff, to be exact.'

Tim Jackson was seldom lost for words but the reply had taken him by surprise. He leaned over Healy.

'Did I hear you right, Mr Healy?'

'You surely did,' Jefferson Healy nodded, removed his top hat and then pulled a key from his vest pocket. He slid the key into the lock of the office door and turned it. The sound of clicking filled both their ears as Healy pushed the door inward and entered.

Jackson trailed the mayor into the office. It

did not have the musty smell the cowboy had expected. He watched as Healy raised the door and window-blinds and allowed the bright sunlight to enter.

The cowboy shuffled around the office and ran his gloved finger across the desk top. It was not dusty. He rested a hip on the edge of the wooden desk and watched as Healy puffed up his chest as he gazed out at the street.

'You trying to look like a real lucky rooster, Mr Healy?' he asked the elegant man. 'I never seen a man look quite so pleased with himself as you do. How come?'

Healy gripped the Havana in the corner of his mouth and grinned at the cowboy.

'You've saved the day, boy,' he said. 'It's as if you were sent from Heaven. We need a lawman and here you are. I've seen a lot of men in my time, but none that seems to fit the bill as well as you do.'

'I ain't accepted the job yet,' Jackson whispered.

'Why ever not?' Healy grinned. 'We need a sheriff and you need a job. You're broke and I pay top dollar.'

Jackson removed his hat and hung it from his holstered six-shooter. 'What is "top dollar", Mr Healy? I'm used to getting twenty dollars a month as a wrangler. Being a star-packer seems a tad more dangerous.'

Healy strode up to the cowboy.

'I'll pay you triple that sum, Tim boy,' he said.

'Sixty a month?' Jackson gasped.

Healy nodded his head slowly without ever taking his eyes from the cowboy. 'That's right. A mighty fair sum if you ask me. What do you think?'

Jackson shrugged. 'Sounds too good to be true.'

'It is true.' Healy patted the muscular arm of the seated cowboy. It was an action he regretted. His fingers felt as though they had just collided with a stone wall.

Jackson tilted his head. 'Any chance of an advance?'

'No problem. Here.' Healy pulled a twenty-dollar bill from his coat pocket and handed it to the cowboy. He then moved around the desk and opened one of the drawers and found a tin star. He handed it to Jackson. 'Pin that on your shirt, Tim boy. You're now the sheriff of Broken Lance.'

Jackson carefully pinned the star to his shirt as he had been instructed. When he looked up the jovial Healy had vanished from the office. The cowboy stood and scratched his head.

'It looks like I've got me a job and a real

handsome salary to go with it,' he muttered to himself as he walked back to the door and looked out into the sun-drenched street. He noticed the townsfolk starting to venture out from their various dwellings. They glanced at the tall cowboy and the star pinned to his chest. It made Jackson even more anxious.

CHAPTER THREE

Joe Lever pushed the bristles of the saloon brush to the edge of the boardwalk and then looked up at the high-shouldered man standing in the doorway of the sheriff's office. Lever straightened up and stared at the tin star pinned to the big man's shirt. The sun danced across the surface of the star as the barman rubbed his neck thoughtfully.

He glanced at the familiar shape of Jefferson Healy as he made his way down the long street toward the small café on the corner. Lever returned his attention to Jackson and then carried his broom back into the Rattler Saloon. The barman discarded the broom as he made his way beyond the horseshoe-shaped counter towards one of the doors on the back wall. He headed to the middle door and turned its brass handle.

The bartender ascended the wooden steps up to

the landing and then marched toward the private suite. He rapped his knuckles across the painted surface of the door and then entered the first of three rooms.

Lever allowed the door to close behind him and watched as a hand rose up from a large bed and released the window blind. The blind rotated upwards and continued to spin as the morning sunlight flooded the room.

'This better be good, Joe,' a growling voice muttered menacingly from somewhere among the tangled blankets. 'You interrupted me and I don't cotton to being interrupted.'

Joe Lever stepped forward. Sweat ran down his face as his eyes adjusted to the glare coming into the room from the street.

'Old Healy has hired himself a new star-packer, boss,' the thin man said. 'I just caught me a glimpse of the critter over in the sheriff's office. Standing proud with that tin star pinned on his chest.'

Buren Ely rose up in the bed and stared at the bartender.

'Healy has done what?' he growled.

'He's hired a new sheriff.' Lever repeated his news.

Ely swung his legs over the edge of the mattress and placed them on the bare floor-boards. His head tilted as his bloodshot eyes burned into Lever.

'That old man will be the death of me,' Ely snorted before turning and staring at the naked female crawling around in the bed sheets behind his hairy back. 'The last thing Broken Lance needs is another damn lawman. We keep killing the critters and Healy keeps on hiring replacements.'

Lever turned his eyes to the female as the naked Ely stood up and snatched at his pants from a nearby chair.

'This new 'un is big, boss,' he said. 'I never seen a man quite so big. Must be close to seven feet tall, if he's an inch.'

Ely looked at Lever. 'Nobody is that big, Joe.'

'This *hombre* is,' Lever insisted.

The female crawled across the bed and reached out at the half-dressed Ely. Her fingers were long and grasping, but seemingly aimless as they sought out something to grab on to.

'Come back to bed, Buren,' she slurred.

'Drink this.' Ely pushed her back and then picked up a half-consumed bottle from a cabinet and tossed it at her. She looked at the bottle and smiled before pulling its cork and raising it to her lips. Her hollow eyes rolled back in her head as she fell against the soiled pillows, clutching the bottle to her breasts.

The bartender looked at Ely.

'What is that?' he asked innocently.

'Liquid heaven, Joe,' Ely grunted. 'Keeps the fillies like Katie here floating in Paradise until the monsters come back visiting. Once they've tasted the stuff they're putty in your hands.'

Lever looked confused. 'Liquid heaven?'

'Laudanum, Joe,' Ely grunted as he cast his scarlet stare down at the female. She made no effort to conceal her once beautiful assets from the bartender. Every inhibition had long gone when Ely had plied her with her first taste of the morphine-laced drink.

'Ain't that addictive, boss?' Lever asked as his eyes were drawn to Katie's writhing body.

Ely spat at the floor. 'I sure hope so. I've got every damn bitch in town hooked on it. They'll do anything just to get another bottle of the stuff.'

Joe Lever fell quiet as he vainly tried to avert his eyes.

'Where'd this giant come from, Joe?' Ely grunted.

Lever returned his eyes to his boss and shrugged.

'Beats the hell out of me! He must have rode in real early, boss. There's a long-limbed grey tied up outside the sheriff's office that must belong to him.'

'Healy must get up before the roosters to catch himself dumb drifters and pin stars on their vests,' Ely raged as he opened the window beside the bed and extracted his manhood from his long underwear. The sound of golden raindrops echoed around the room before Ely had emptied his bladder. He shook himself and then returned it to its soiled hiding-place.

Buren Ely buttoned his trouser fly and pulled up his suspenders over his stained long johns top. He snatched a shirt and put it on before lifting his heavy twin-holstered gun belt. He buckled the leather shooting rig and advanced toward his underling.

'Hell, they ain't had time to bury the last star-toting bastard we killed, Joe. Healy is sure getting to be a nuisance,' he growled.

'Maybe we oughta kill Healy instead of the varmints he keeps hiring, boss?' Lever suggested as the stout Ely marched out toward the stairs.

As he reached the top of the staircase, Ely paused and glanced at Lever.

'This young star-packer … he's big, you say?' he queried.

Lever nodded firmly. 'Yep, he's big OK. Mighty big.'

Ely rubbed his unkempt face.

'Good. That'll make him a whole lot easier to kill when the lead starts flying.'

Both men made their way down the steps.

As they entered the heart of the saloon Ely snapped his fingers at the barman. 'Rustle up the rest of the boys, Joe. I want them here in case that high-shouldered *hombre* happens to be good at being a lawman.'

Joe Lever ran across the fresh sawdust and out through the swing doors. Ely made his way behind the horseshoe counter and plucked a whiskey bottle off a shelf and filled a beer glass with its amber contents.

He took a big swallow and shook like a wet hound.

'Nothing and nobody is gonna ruin my plans,' he vowed.

CHAPTER FOUR

The fact that the sheriff's office appeared to be far cleaner than Jackson could fathom was still gnawing at the young lawman's craw as he made his way along the main street leading his grey stallion behind his wide back. He began to notice that more and more of the townsfolk were appearing from their respective dwellings and beginning their daily rituals.

Jackson glanced around the street at the buildings. Broken Lance had no collective style. Every one of the structures was different to the next. It seemed curious to the high-shouldered young lawman, but that was not what was troubling him.

His thoughts kept returning to the fact that in less than five minutes of riding into the sprawling settlement he had been hired as sheriff.

He walked up to the tall, wide-open doors of the livery stable with his grey in tow and stopped beside the glowing forge. His eyes darted around the interior of the stable as he noticed the horse-flesh filling nearly all of its stalls.

The tall man dropped his long leathers and rested his wrists on his holstered Colt .45s. He had never before seen so many horses in a livery stable at the same time.

Suddenly, a sound above him caught Jackson's attention. He swung on his heels and drew one of his guns and cocked its hammer.

'Don't you go firing that hogleg, mister!' A grizzled voice floated down from the hay-loft as a muscular man peered down at him.

Jackson sighed heavily and released the hammer. He straightened up and returned the weapon to its holster as his eyes watched the man start down the ladder.

'My apologies! You kinda spooked me, mister,' admitted Jackson.

The greasy blacksmith reached the hay-strewn floor of the stable and turned to face Jackson. He gave a nod of approval as he noticed the star on the younger man's shirt.

'So, *you* must be the new sheriff,' he noted as he

walked toward the grey and rested the palm of his hand on the horse's head. 'Where'd old Healy find you?'

Jackson raised an eyebrow. 'Jefferson Healy tends to make a habit of hiring new sheriffs, I take it?'

The blacksmith nodded as he stroked the neck of the grey and studied Jackson carefully.

'You might say that, Sheriff,' he said.

Jackson nodded thoughtfully. 'Just how many new sheriffs has Healy appointed?'

'You must be the second this month.' The blacksmith led the grey to an empty stall and began to remove his saddle from the horse's back.

Jackson placed a hand on a wooden upright and accepted his bedroll from the busy man.

'What happened to the last star-packer?' he asked.

The blacksmith paused and turned to look up at Jackson's face. He forced a smile.

'He died.'

Jackson rolled his eyes. 'I figured that much. How did he die?'

'He tangled with a few of Buren Ely's hired guns,' the blacksmith said dryly. 'It don't pay to get on the wrong side of Ely, Sheriff.'

The colour drained from Jackson's face as he pondered the information he had just been given. The newly appointed lawman wandered to the forge and stared into the glowing coals. As the burly blacksmith walked from the horse Jackson tilted his head.

'Who the Hell is this Ely critter?' Jackson questioned.

'He's trouble, boy.'

Jackson tucked the bedroll under his arm and looked hard at the blacksmith. He knew that the friendly man was hiding more than he was willing to reveal. He wondered why.

'Tell me everything you know about this Ely critter,' Jackson said firmly. 'What's his business and why don't he like lawmen?'

The blacksmith sat on the side of the forge. He looked at the livery stable floor for a few moments and then looked up at the towering Jackson.

'My name's Griff,' he said.

'My name's Tim,' Jackson nodded. 'I need to know why Ely has his hired guns kill star-packers. I don't hanker dying due to ignorance, Griff.'

'Ely is bad news, Sheriff,' Griff began. 'He rode into Broken Lance two summers back with a handful of hired guns and a wagon full of whores.

The old town ain't bin the same since.'

Jackson rubbed his jawline. 'And he started having the town's lawmen killed?'

Griff shook his head. 'Not at first. That only started about six months ago. For some reason Ely's men began to kill anyone who wore a star.'

Jackson frowned. 'Just how many star-packers has Ely had killed, Griff?'

'Four before you.' The blacksmith rested his hands on his knees and stared at the grey stallion. 'If I was you I'd saddle that horse back up after he's rested and ride out of here. It ain't healthy around Broken Lance for anyone wearing a star.'

Jackson stretched up to his full height.

'I don't scare that easy. I'll hang around until I've got me a reason for all these killings, Griff.'

The blacksmith stood up and squared himself before the youngster. He continued to shake his head.

'Get out of town while you still can, Tim boy,' he urged. 'The graveyard is full of dead heroes. You're too young to join that club.'

The newly hired lawman did not show any signs of being either afraid or troubled by the words of the older man. All he seemed to be was curious as to why Ely was having his gun hands kill the town's lawmen.

'Where does Ely tend to frequent, friend?' Jackson asked in a low drawl.

For the longest time the blacksmith did not answer. He stared up at the high-shouldered lawman until he realized that Jackson was not the kind to just turn tail and run.

'He owns the Rattler Saloon,' Griff finally answered. 'Hardly ever shows his face out of there, though. He's got at least a dozen whores working shifts in that cesspit and he knows every single one of them personally.'

'Shouldn't be too hard to find him, then,' Jackson sighed.

'It's his hired gunmen you gotta look out for, though, boy. They're spread all around town waiting to do whatever their boss tells them.' The blacksmith added in warning, 'Back-shooters, the whole bunch of them.'

'I'll keep my eyes peeled for those *hombres*,' Jackson said before drying his brow on his shirt sleeve.

'Heed my words, Tim,' Griff urged. 'This town ain't worth getting killed in.'

Jackson patted the shoulder of the blacksmith.

'I'm obliged for the information and the

warning, Griff,' he said thoughtfully. 'I'll think on it.'

The blacksmith watched as the young lawman strode back out into the blazing morning sun. He sat back down on the edge of the forge and stared at the ground angrily. He pounded his fists on his knees.

'Damn it all!' he cursed sorrowfully. 'He should have listened!'

CHAPTER FIVE

Rex Carter steered his sweat-laden mount around the rear of the buildings and kept to the back alleyways until he had reached his goal. The horseman drew back on his long leathers and guided the weary animal up to the rear entrance of a red, brick structure and then dismounted.

The rear of the building gave no clue as to what business was undertaken within its sturdy walls. There was none of the bright paint which adorned the front of the structure. Only grime and a decade of neglect covered its walls.

Carter looped his reins around a porch upright and secured his horse before stepping up to the unkempt door. His gloved knuckles rapped across its weathered surface until he heard movement behind the wooden door.

The sound of bolts being released filled the

narrow confines of the alley just before the door was eased open. The eyes of both men met as Carter was silently admitted.

The door was bolted behind the gunman before he trailed the brutish man down a long dark corridor toward the light in the heart of the building. Carter watched with narrowed eyes as his hefty guide pushed the door into the small office. He shouldered his way past the guard and stared at the crumpled figure sat behind his desk amid a mountain of books and papers. Only the blue line of rising cigar smoke gave any hint that the aged man sat behind the desk was still alive.

Carter moved to a chair opposite the seated man and sat down. He rested his elbows on the arms of the wooden chair and clasped his gloved hands together just below his unshaven chin.

The watery eyes of the elderly creature rose and stared at Carter for a few moments. Then a trembling hand removed the thin cigar from his wrinkled lips and tapped ash onto an already mountainous pile of ash.

The deathly old man leaned back in his chair and studied Carter as if he did not recognize the gunman. Yet both men had known one another for the better part of two years.

'Why are you here, Carter?' the old man asked before returning the cigar to his mouth.

'You told me to keep my eyes open for any strangers that happened to be headed this way, boss,' Carter answered as his eyes darted around the claustrophobic office. 'You told me to report to you as soon as someone showed. Well, someone showed.'

Pontious Longshank stared through the cigar smoke at his hired gunman. There was no hint of any emotion in his aged face as he absorbed Carter's words.

'Who showed?' he finally enquired.

Carter leaned forward on his chair and looked across the papers at his paymaster.

'A mighty big *hombre*, boss.' Carter raised one of his hands and tried to indicate how big the drifter was. 'I never seen anyone as tall as this critter. Whoever he is, he headed down into Broken Lance and I trailed him here. I kept to the back streets so I wouldn't be spotted. That's what you told me to do, didn't you?'

'Exactly!' Longshank gave a slight nod of his ancient head and added to the pile of cigar ash. 'Apart from being tall, what exactly did the rider look like?'

Carter rubbed his chin. 'He looked kinda young.'

Longshank sat forward and brushed aside a pile of papers until his watery eyes had a clear view of his henchman. 'You say he looked young? Exactly how young?'

'Maybe thirty,' Carter shrugged. 'Maybe less. It's hard to tell with them really big *hombres*. He was wearing two guns in fancy holsters.'

'Would you say he's a cowboy?' Longshank pressed.

'He might be,' the gunman conceded. 'But I never seen a cowpoke wearing twin guns in expensive holsters before, boss.'

The gunman watched as Longshank brooded behind the cloud of cigar smoke that shrouded his head. He had never seen the old man quite so concerned before and it troubled the hired killer.

'What's all this about, boss?' he finally asked. 'You've bin like a cat on a hot tin roof for the past month. It ain't like you. Who are you expecting?'

Longshank cast his eyes on the gunman.

'I'm expecting trouble, Carter.' He sighed. 'Really big trouble.'

Carter pointed at the wall. 'Are you telling me that tall critter who rode into Broken Lance is the trouble you're expecting?'

Longshank rose to his feet and shuffled around the desk. A cloud of smoke hung in the office marking the route he was taking. The aged man stopped by a desk and plucked up a whiskey bottle and two dusty glasses. He returned to his seat and rested his bones back down upon it.

Carter watched as his paymaster pulled the cork and filled both glasses with the amber liquor. He leaned across the pile of papers and lifted one of the glasses.

'You didn't answer me, boss,' Carter said as he lifted the glass to his lips and took a sip of the powerful whiskey. 'Is that young *hombre* the fella you've bin telling me to keep an eye open for?'

Longshank downed his whiskey in one swift action. His eyes returned to the hired gunman.

'He might be.'

Carter continued to sip his drink as Longshank refilled his own glass.

'What do you mean?' he asked. 'He either is or he ain't.'

Longshank reached into the inside pocket of his jacket and pulled out a folded note. He tossed it at the gunman.

'Read that,' he ordered.

Carter rested his glass on the papers and unfolded the scrap of paper. The message upon it was brief but troubling.

I'm sending my top gun to town, Longshank. He'll kill you unless you pay him the money you cheated me out of.
K.

Carter lowered the letter after reading its contents and stared at the old man as he again downed his whiskey in one easy throw.

Longshank sighed. 'For twenty years I've bin waiting for that letter, Carter. Twenty years, and out of the blue I get that.'

'Who is this "K" varmint?' Carter asked as he handed the note back to its owner.

'Keno,' Longshank said bitterly. 'We used to be partners but then he ended up going to prison. I figured he must be dead by now. Reckon I was wrong.'

'You owe him some money?' Carter finished his drink.

Longshank shrugged his bony shoulders. 'After he went to prison I sold the business and headed west with the proceeds, Carter. Seems as if Keno figures I owe him a share.'

'Do you?'

The elderly man just nodded.

Carter pushed his hat back until it rested on the crown of his head. 'So that young fella is here to collect?'

'I reckon so.'

Carter pushed his empty glass toward the bottle and watched as Longshank filled both tumblers. The gunman lifted the glass and smiled at the thoughtful older man.

'The letter says that he's sending his top gun, boss,' he started. 'That means the tall *hombre* is pretty handy with his guns.'

'That seems kinda obvious,' Longshank said as he stared at the whiskey in his glass. 'What are you getting at?'

'A bonus,' Carter grinned. 'If I kill that young fella I want two hundred bucks bonus on top of my wages.'

Longshank looked through his watery eyes and nodded.

'You kill him and I'll pay you double that, Carter,' he hissed. 'If this stranger is one of Keno's top men, then you'll earn every damn cent.'

Carter got to his feet, finished his drink and

went to turn. The gunman paused for a brief moment and glanced at his frail employer.

'I ain't afeared of that tall drink of water, boss,' he drawled as he touched his hat brim. 'The bigger they are, the harder they fall.'

Pontious Longshank watched as the seasoned hired gun departed his small office. He shuffled papers and then filled his glass once again.

He wanted to run but it had been a long time since his legs had been capable of obeying him. Longshank lifted the glass to his lined lips.

'If that bastard Keno figures that I'm gonna pay his top gun a single penny, he's mistaken.' The elderly man downed his drink and stared at the empty glass in his twisted fingers. 'I'll take my fortune with me to the grave rather than buckle to any threats. He ain't getting nuthin'.'

The ponderous sound of hefty footsteps drew Longshank's attention. He looked up to the door and watched as it opened again.

The hideous guard had returned to the office just as Rex Carter was exiting by the rear door of the building. The large man rested his hairy left hand on the office door-frame as he stared at Longshank thoughtfully.

'Everything OK, boss?' he asked. 'You look

kinda spooked to me.'

Longshank pondered the question as he focused on the brutish creature bathed in the vague shafts of sunlight which managed to penetrate the small room.

'Go get your scattergun and keep it close, Bruno,' he advised. 'And make sure you got plenty of shells.'

Bruno Taska pushed his limp greasy mane of hair off his brutalized face and looked hard at his boss. His head tilted.

'We expecting trouble, boss?' he grunted.

Longshank raised his wrinkled head and forced a half-hearted smile at his bodyguard.

'Maybe,' he sighed.

Bruno nodded. 'I'll get my scattergun.'

CHAPTER SIX

The town's streets were filling up fast as the heat of a new day drew its citizens out into the growing sunlight. The eyes of the high-shouldered young sheriff darted around him as he slowly proceeded down the main street. Jackson was confused by Broken Lance. He had never before ridden into a place which suddenly gave him a high-priced job before.

Jackson knew that he should be thankful, but there was something nagging at his every sinew. He paused just outside a hardware store as its owner stacked a selection of his wares on the boardwalk.

The lawman rubbed his neck with the palm of his hand and watched the people who also watched him. They were obviously curious at the sight of a stranger wearing a tin star. Jackson was just curious.

The words of the blacksmith haunted him.

His eyes glanced along the boardwalk to the Rattler Saloon. Buren Ely was a secretive man, according to Griff at the livery stable.

Secretive and dangerous.

Griff had said that he was behind the killing of several of the town's lawmen. Jackson wondered why and was curious to know if he might be the next to get gunned down.

The notion chilled him.

Jackson rested a muscular shoulder against the store upright as his narrowed eyes studied the street. Men, women and children passed in all directions. They were like so many others he had seen over the years. They covered the entire spectrum of people. Poor, not so poor, and well-heeled.

The scent of cooking filled his nostrils.

Jackson felt his stomach remind him that it was empty. He rubbed his flat belly and heard the store-owner stop just behind him. As his eyes spotted the small café set amongst the buildings opposite his attention was alerted by an unexpected voice behind him.

'Are you the new sheriff, son?'

Jackson stood away from the upright, turned and glanced down at the stocky man with an apron stretched around his wide girth. He gave a nod as the man's baggy eyes looked at the tin star pinned to Jackson's shirt.

'Yep, I'm the new sheriff,' Jackson smiled.

The hardware store owner shook his head and tutted sadly before placing a hand on Jackson's arm.

'I'm sure sorry to hear that, son,' he sighed. 'You look like such a nice boy. It's a crying shame you're wearing that star.'

Jackson raised an eyebrow and watched the man step back into his store. 'Nice to have met you.'

Resting his hands on his gun grips, Jackson was about to step down from the boardwalk and cross the road when he was aware of horses trotting down the street. He turned to his left and watched five horses and their riders approach.

Jackson watched the roughshod horsemen as they passed. His head twisted as he observed them continue on through the busy street. When the horses pulled up outside the Rattler, the sheriff realized who they were.

They were some of the hired gunmen that Griff had told him about. Jackson focused hard on the men as they swiftly dismounted and headed into the saloon.

He exhaled and then rubbed his neck again.

Jackson stepped down onto the sand and crossed the wide thoroughfare toward the café. The aroma of cooking grew stronger as he closed the distance between the petite building and his nostrils.

The lawman stepped up onto the boardwalk, tipped his hat at a few passing females and then entered the café. He removed his Stetson and looked around the empty interior of the small business.

A handsome female appeared from the back of the café.

Their eyes met.

Without realizing it, they both smiled.

She looked at the star on his shirt and then approached the tall man.

'So you're the new sheriff?' she said as she invited him to sit down with a wave of her hand. 'Old Healy is getting faster at hiring you guys. The last one is still lying in the funeral parlour.'

Jackson absorbed her words and then sat down on a hard chair. He placed his hat on the chair next to him.

'My name's Jackson, ma'am,' he said. 'Tim Jackson. I'm mighty pleased to make your acquaintance.'

Unexpectedly, she seated herself opposite the lawman. There was genuine concern in her handsome face.

'My name's Peg,' she informed, then added quickly, 'Damned if I know why I told you that, Tim.'

Jackson stared into her blue eyes – eyes which were framed by the most luxurious black eyelashes he had ever seen. 'What do you mean, Peg?'

She stood back up. 'You'll be dead before I get time to know you. Star-packers tend to draw lead like outhouses draw flies – especially around here.'

A hint of a smile etched his face.

'You sound kinda upset at the thought of us not getting acquainted, Peg,' he wryly noted.

Peg Smith rested her hands on her hips and sighed.

'Ham and eggs?'

The newly appointed lawman nodded.

Peg turned and started back to the rear of the café. She had only taken three steps when she turned her slim neck and looked back at the fresh-faced sheriff.

'I'm deadly serious, Tim,' she said. 'If you keep wearing that star they'll kill you. As sure as night follows day, they'll kill you.'

He looked at her concerned face. 'Does that sadden you, Peg? Am I the kinda guy you'd like to wrestle with?'

'You ain't gonna live long enough to know the answer to that!' she replied hastily before turning away from him and continuing on to the cooking range. 'Not if you keep wearing that damn tin star.'

The smiling Jackson turned his chair and stared out through the window at the sun-drenched street. He rested his hands on his holsters.

'I reckon I already know,' he whispered under his breath as he concentrated on the horses tied up outside the Rattler Saloon. 'It'd be nice to find out for sure, though.'

CHAPTER SEVEN

The Cattleman Club drew its private members from hundreds of miles in all directions. The men within the well-established club did the exact same things that their poorer neighbours did. They drank hard liquor, gambled their fortunes and spent time with willing females less than half their ages. The only difference was that they did it in private, within the hallowed walls of their exclusive club.

Jefferson Healy signed the register and moved from the lobby into the library. He touched his hat brim to all of his fellow members and made his way to his favourite chair.

He had no sooner sat down than one of the waiters brought him his regular morning tipple of brandy and milk. He accepted the drink and unfolded his newspaper.

As he sipped at his drink he noticed two of his

oldest friends move toward him. The scent of their cigars reached him a few moments before they did.

'You're earlier than usual, Healy.'

The mayor of Broken Lance lowered his paper and looked up at the jovial face above him. He stared at both Dawson Brooks and Quentin Vale as they rested their elbows on the ornate mantle beside his chair.

'I did rise a few hours earlier this morning,' Healy said before pulling out his pocket-watch and checking the time. 'Come to think of it, I ain't even had breakfast yet.'

Vale leaned over. 'They've got sweetbread. The chef told me when I arrived.'

Healy nodded. 'That sounds mighty good.'

Brooks pointed his cigar at Healy. 'You've been up to something, Healy. I know that impish grin. What have you up and done?'

'I hired a new sheriff for the town, gentlemen,' boasted Healy. 'This one looks the part. A really tall fella if ever I've seen one.'

Both Brooks and Vale looked down at the mayor. They seemed less enthusiastic than Healy. The two men drew their chairs closer to their friend and sat down on either side of him.

'Are you sure that's wise, Healy?' Brooks asked,

concern etched on his face.

Vale shook his head. 'I think it's playing with fire.'

Healy looked at their troubled faces and then pulled out his silver cigar case. He extracted one of its fat Havanas and bit off its tip.

'What do you mean?' he asked them as he placed the cigar between his teeth and struck a match. 'As mayor of Broken Lance it's my job to hire lawmen.'

'You hire them and certain parties kill them,' Vale noted.

'Unnamed parties,' Brooks added quietly.

Healy puffed on his cigar as his eyes darted between their faces. 'But the town needs a lawman. We all know how important it is that we engage a sheriff at the moment.'

'But hiring new lawmen will only rile a certain party in Broken Lance, Healy,' Brooks pointed out. 'He might get angry with us if you keep hiring new lawmen to replace the ones he's already had killed.'

Healy frowned. 'Buren Ely has to be stopped.'

'He's too powerful, Healy,' Vale sighed.

'The right sheriff will stop him,' the mayor insisted. 'I think I've hired the right man this time.

He's as tall as a tree and sports a hand-tooled gun belt with two holsters. This critter can stop our friend Ely in his tracks.'

Both men shook their heads as cigar smoke encircled them.

Healy tossed his newspaper at the ground and sat upright in his easy chair. He shook his fist at the pair.

'Ely has been adding to his private army over the last few months. I'm told he has a dozen or more hired guns on his payroll and we know why.'

Brooks looked at Healy. 'Even Ely wouldn't dare to try and do what you're suggesting. It would take the US army to do what you think Ely is planning. It's impossible.'

'Mark my words,' snorted Healy. 'Ely is gonna try and do the impossible. Think about it. If he manages to pull off this job, he'll be the richest man in the territory.'

'And you've hired a new sheriff to try and stop him?' Brooks sighed. 'One man against Ely and his army of thugs. The poor fool will be in a box headed for Boot Hill before sundown.'

Healy finished his drink and pushed his cigar into the corner of his mouth. He abruptly stood up and looked at his friends with distain.

'I'm surprised at your attitude!' he snapped. 'I bid you goodbye.'

They too stood.

'Where are you going?' Brooks enquired.

'They'll be serving breakfast soon,' Vale added.

Jefferson Healy could not conceal his disappointment or his anger. 'I'm going to my office where I can brood on the fact that I might just have hired a man simply to watch him get killed.'

'Don't get riled, Healy,' Brooks shrugged.

'If someone doesn't stop Buren Ely we'll all be a whole lot poorer than we are right now.' Healy nodded firmly at them. 'At least I'm trying to stop him. I might fail but at least I'm gonna try.'

The entire membership of the Cattleman Club watched as the mayor collected his hat and stormed back out into the sun-baked street.

CHAPTER EIGHT

One question kept burning into Jackson's mind as he strolled around the busy streets of Broken Lance. It was like a branding iron that would not quit. Why would a saloon owner surround his sorrowful hide with so many gunmen and keep having them kill star-packers?

He had walked down every alley and side street in town before he finally returned to the long main street. Jackson rested his broad shoulders against a corner wall and allowed his eyes to continue to journey along its length.

Even the shade provided by the porch he rested beneath could not cool him. It was hotter than Hell, and going to get hotter. His eyes focused on a large clock in the window of a jeweller's store across the street. It was still not even noon.

He looked down at the shining star on his shirt

front.

It might as well be a bull's-eye pinned to his chest, he thought. He glanced down the street at the Rattler. There were more horses tethered to its hitching rails now. His large hand rubbed his neck.

Jackson began to wonder why so many of the townsfolk had been warning him off. None of them could have made it any clearer. Being a lawman in this town was the same as being a man sentenced to die.

His eyes drifted along the store fronts and stopped when they reached the café. His head tilted as he watched the handsome female who had rustled up his breakfast.

'There you are.'

Jackson turned and looked down at the well-attired mayor as he crossed the street carefully. He moved quickly for an older man with a big belly, the sheriff thought.

'Howdy, Mayor!' Jackson greeted Healy again.

The mayor stopped next to the tall sheriff and looked up at his troubled expression.

'Something eating at you, boy?' he asked.

Jackson nodded. 'Yep.'

Healy looked all around them and was thankful

that the town's numerous inhabitants shielded them from the prying eyes of Ely's gunmen. The mayor grabbed the forearm of the sheriff and tugged it.

'Come with me, Tim boy,' he instructed.

Jackson remained rooted to the spot. 'Where to?'

'My office.' Healy led his tall young friend through the crowd and turned into Baker Street. With his hands resting upon his gun grips the well-constructed lawman trailed the mayor down the side street.

Healy led Jackson up the stone steps and into the red-brick structure. Jackson watched as the mayor locked the front door and then turned into an office.

It was much cooler inside the building and Jackson was grateful. He sat down opposite Healy across a fine mahogany desk. The lawman watched as the stocky man filled two glasses with water and reached across to hand one to Jackson.

Healy looked troubled as he sipped at the water.

Jackson emptied his glass in three swallows and placed it onto the desk. He leaned back in his chair and looked around the office.

'Why'd you want me to come here with you,

Mayor?' he asked. 'Is it because every damn varmint that pins a star on gets himself shot?'

Healy exhaled and placed his cigar into a glass ashtray.

'So you've heard,' he said.

'Yep,' Jackson nodded. 'I heard.'

Healy rested his elbows on the desk. 'OK. The job is dangerous. I admit that. But you must have figured that when you accepted the star.'

Jackson removed his hat and balanced it on his knees. 'I knew that wearing a star is dangerous, Mayor. The thing is you forgot to warn me just how dangerous it is.'

'We've had some bad luck.' Healy fanned his hands.

'And that bad luck usually comes from the guns of Ely's gunmen,' Jackson added. 'I've bin told that quite a few of your sheriffs have ended up dead.'

'Who told you that?'

'Just about everyone who's spotted this star has told me the same thing.' Jackson tapped the star with his thumb. 'Folks are mighty talkative in Broken Lance and they all kinda agree that it just ain't healthy walking around with one of these on your chest.'

At that, Healy looked sheepish.

'Being a lawman is never a healthy profession, Tim,' he shrugged.

Jackson grinned. 'I know that. The thing is, here in Broken Lance it's almost suicidal.'

'You want to quit?' The mayor pulled out his pocket-watch and checked the time. 'Hell, I only hired you two hours ago.'

Jackson got back to his feet and placed his Stetson back on his head. He ambled to the window and stared out at the sunlit street for a few moments before turning to stare at the older man.

'There's something bigger in this story that you ain't letting on about, Mayor,' he said. 'You seem intent on hiring men to fill the post of sheriff even though they get themselves shot pretty soon after pinning the star on.'

Healy swallowed hard.

Jackson marched across the office and pointed an accusing finger at the seated man.

'Why is it so darned important that you got yourself a lawman, Mayor?' the younger man pressed. 'Tell me the truth or I will up and quit.'

Jefferson Healy leaned hard against his padded backrest and looked into the eyes of the far taller man. He exhaled and shook his head solemnly.

'OK, Tim. I reckon I owe you that,' he admitted.

Jackson rested a hip on the corner of the desk. 'I'm listening, so start talking.'

The mayor took a deep breath and then began to tell his latest sheriff why he was so desperate to have a lawman in his town at all costs.

'Four years ago up the valley they built a smelter,' Healy revealed. 'A *gold* smelter.'

Jackson frowned. 'There ain't no gold around here. Is there?'

Healy raised a finger. 'Not exactly. But up the valley there are a few gold-mines. For years they just scratched a living finding the odd gold nugget and some dust.'

The high-shouldered sheriff raised an eyebrow.

'Then someone hit paydirt?' he asked.

Healy nodded. 'They hit the motherload, son. So much ore that they couldn't ship it all out to get it refined. So my friends at the Cattleman Club got a company floated on the stock market back east. We built a smelter to handle all the refined gold into bricks.'

Jackson looked impressed. 'Golden bricks?'

'Yep,' Healy nodded. 'Golden bricks. They've got more than a hundred of them under lock and key in a warehouse next to the refinery.'

'I still don't understand why you need a sheriff

so badly, Mayor,' Jackson admitted. 'Surely you don't expect me to guard all that gold. Or do you?'

'Nope.' Healy stood and grabbed the arms of his protégé. 'They've got those gold bricks protected by a dozen guards up in the valley.'

'Then why do you need a star-packer?' Jackson wondered.

'The warehouse is nearly full,' Healy continued his story. 'They've got to transport it from the safety of the warehouse to the mint in Austin, boy. It'll be vulnerable whilst it's on the road.'

Jackson rubbed his jaw. 'That's why Ely has bin killing the lawmen around here. Without the law to protect that valuable cargo, he can do what he wants.'

'And what he wants is to steal every damn bar of gold they ship off to Austin,' Healy nodded. 'Don't you see? If we let Buren Ely get his hands on that shipment, he'll be the richest man in the damn country.'

'How much is that gold worth?'

'More than either of us can imagine,' the mayor said. 'It might be millions. I don't know.'

Tim Jackson rubbed his neck and sighed, 'Holy smoke!'

Healy watched as the high-shouldered young-ster paced around the room like a caged puma. He said nothing until Jackson returned to the desk and leaned over him.

'How does this concern you exactly, Mayor?' he asked.

'I'm a shareholder in the company,' Healy replied. 'If anything happens to that first load of gold bricks before it arrives at the mint, a thousand other shareholders will be mighty sore. Plus I'll lose everything I've got. I invested my life savings in that company.'

'Just how do you figure one man can stop a herd of armed robbers?' Jackson asked.

Healy patted the muscular arm of the sheriff. 'You've got the law on your side, Tim. You've got the power of the law behind you.'

'Can I hire deputies?' Jackson asked.

Healy nodded. 'If you can find anyone willing to square up to Ely and his vermin I'll pay their salary.'

Jackson stretched up to his full height.

'Reckon I'll not retire just yet, Mayor,' he smiled.

Healy watched as Jackson checked both his six-shooters and then headed toward the office doorway. The mayor studied the wide back of the youngster as Jackson turned the door handle and pulled the door toward him.

'You're staying in Broken Lance after what I've just told you, Tim?' he asked in disbelief.

Jackson paused and glanced across the office.

'Somebody took a couple of shots at me up on the hillside, Mayor,' Jackson said thoughtfully. 'If nothing else, I intend finding out why.'

Healy pushed himself away from his desk and crossed the room to the tall figure. 'What about Ely and the gold?'

Jackson smiled. 'I'm considering that.'

The mayor could not conceal his glee. 'I knew you were the right man for the job as soon as I set eyes on you, son. The sort of man born to wear a star.'

The high-shouldered sheriff raised his eyebrows.

'I don't know about that but there's a mighty handsome woman working down at the café yonder and I figured I oughta try and get to know her a little better,' Jackson admitted. 'She sure looks like she might be amiable.' He winked.

'You mean the young widow woman?' Healy asked.

'Called herself Peg.'

Healy nodded. 'That's her. Peggy Smith.'

'How come she's a widow, Mayor?' Jackson asked. 'She's kinda young to have lost a husband.'

'Ely's boys killed young Tom Smith in cold blood,' Healy sighed sadly. 'Without a sheriff, we couldn't do a damn thing.'

Jackson's face stiffened as he gritted his teeth. 'No wonder she advised me to quit being a star-packer and get the hell out of town.'

'What you thinking about, Tim?'

'I'm thinking about a little lady who has bin wronged,' Jackson said. 'I'm also thinking about Ely and that gold. It's all tangled up together as I see it.'

'What you going to do?' Healy wondered.

'I'm gonna try and right that wrong, Mayor.' Jackson pulled the brim of his Stetson down to shield his eyes as he marched back out toward the bright street.

For the first time in a long while Jefferson Healy felt there was a slim chance that Broken Lance might be on the verge of finally ridding itself of the evil which was threatening to destroy it.

The mayor raced to his office window, rested his hands on the glass panes and watched as the lawman strode back toward the main street. Yet for all his faith in those wide shoulders of Jackson's, he knew that the young star-packer was but one man against many.

Healy wondered if he had just sent another good man to his death. The thought gnawed at his innards.

CHAPTER NINE

The Rattler was beginning to fill with men as the hands of its tobacco-stained wall-clock moved ever closer to eleven. Yet the most notorious saloon in Broken Lance would not truly come to life until after sundown. Only then would the soiled doves emerge from their nests and frequent the large interior of the saloon in search of men with the money and time to buy their dubious favours.

Sunlight billowed into the heart of the saloon.

It bathed the patrons of the long bar in its hostile heat as they gathered around the horse-shoe counter and quenched their habitual thirsts with rot-gut whiskey and warm beer.

Joe Lever stared up from the glasses he was filling with whiskey and stared at the massive figure beside the swing doors. The bartender gulped as his eyes tried to focus.

Although it was impossible to see Tim Jackson's features with the bright sun behind him, Lever knew exactly who was standing with his hands upon the tops of the swing doors.

Few men were as tall or as wide as Jackson.

There was none at all in the remote settlement apart from the stranger. Lever accepted the coins and moved towards the cash drawer and dropped them into the wooden compartments as his eyes continued to watch the high-shouldered lawman.

Jackson pushed the doors inward and walked into the Rattler. Each step was slow and deliberate as he made his way across the room towards the counter.

One by one the rest of the men within the saloon looked to where Lever was staring open-mouthed. They too were taken back by the height of the stranger that none of them had ever set eyes upon before.

'You look like you seen the Devil himself, Joe,' one of the customers joked as his humour soon became contagious. The sound of grunting laughter traced a route around the bar counter, but Lever did not laugh. He did not even smile.

All Joe Lever could do was watch the tall man stride across the sawdust-covered floor towards him, and sweat.

The bartender's eyes darted from Jackson's face to the tin star pinned upon his large chest. They returned to the square-jawed face as Jackson reached him.

Jackson glanced to the others who were spread out around the horseshoe bar. His attention then returned to Lever as he placed a hand on the damp surface of the counter and rested a boot on the brass rail.

'What can I do for you, Sheriff?' Lever asked as his customers continued to laugh at him.

Jackson did not answer. He studied the men who were propping up the counter to either side of him carefully. None of them looked as though they were hired gunmen like the men he had been warned about. None of them looked as though they could afford to buy a horse, let alone ride one.

'Where are the men belonging to them horses out front?' he asked slowly.

Lever cleared his throat. 'I don't know.'

Jackson raised an eyebrow and turned his attention to the flight of stairs. He looked up at the landing above them and saw two men move to the banister. Both men were well armed and defiantly stared down at the tall lawman.

'No matter,' Jackson said as his thumbs flicked the safety loops off his gun hammers and rested his palms on the grips of his holstered guns. 'I reckon I already know.'

Joe Lever mopped his brow as he watched the tall figure back away from his counter whilst keeping his eyes glued to the landing.

The saloon suddenly quietened.

'You ain't thinking of using them guns are you, Sheriff?' he asked.

'I'm doing more than think,' Jackson nodded. 'That's why I got hired, friend. I'll kill anyone that even looks like he's thinking of killing me.'

Both men pushed their coat-tails over their guns and moved towards the top of the staircase. They had already been primed by their paymaster with just one order.

When you see anyone wearing a star, kill him.

Jackson continued to move backwards until he was in the centre of the room. He then stopped and raised his hands a couple of inches above his guns.

There was no mistaking the intentions of the pair of hired guns on the landing. They were watching Jackson like two vultures waiting for death.

Suddenly, their patience evaporated. Both men

slapped leather and drew their guns and fanned tier hammers.

As shots rained down at the lawman every customer in the Rattler dived for cover. Sawdust kicked up off the floor as Jackson calmly dragged his six-shooters from their holsters and returned fire.

With red-hot tapers passing within inches of the high-shouldered lawman, Jackson gritted his teeth and fired through the choking gunsmoke.

He watched as one of the gunmen buckled and fell head-first down the stairs as his cohort was punched backwards into a wall and then bounced forward.

Jackson watched the gunman crash through the wooden balustrade and fall like a lead weight. The legs of a card table shattered as the dead gunman landed heavily upon its green baize.

'Tell Ely that's only the beginning,' Jackson warned the bartender. 'I get mighty sore when folks start shooting at me.'

He turned and walked slowly back out into the blazing morning sun. Fearfully, Joe Lever looked over the edge of the bar counter and stared wide-eyed at the swing doors rocking on their hinges.

The barman raced to the private door at the

rear of the Rattler and into the dimly lit way up to Ely's rooms. He had barely reached the steps when Buren Ely emerged above him flanked by most of his hired guns.

'What was that shooting me and the boys heard, Joe?' he shouted at the startled Lever.

The barman raised a hand and pointed into the belly of the saloon. 'That was that big galoot I seen earlier, boss.'

Ely stopped beside the shaking Lever. 'Davis and Parker will deal with him if he's drunk, Joe. Stop shaking.'

Lever moved closer to his boss.

'You don't understand,' he stammered. 'They're dead. Davis and Parker is dead. That big fella just killed them.'

Ely grabbed the collar of the barman and lifted him off the ground. 'What you talking about, Joe? Why would he kill Parker and Davis?'

'They seen the tin star he got pinned to his shirt and they squared up to him,' Lever frantically explained. 'That tall varmint let them draw and then blasted them like he was swatting flies, boss. I never seen such shooting.'

Ely released Lever and rubbed his bloodshot eyes.

'Healy must have told him a few things,' he growled. 'Reckon he figured on shooting first and asking questions later.'

'That star-packer told me to tell you that was just the beginning, boss.' Lever gulped as the rest of the gunmen reached the foot of the concealed steps and gathered around Ely. 'He said he gets real sore when folks start shooting at him.'

Buren Ely shook his head and turned to his small army of cut-throats.

'I don't know who that tall bastard is but I want him dead even worse than I wanted all them other star-packers dead,' he snarled angrily. 'I don't care how you do it but I want him in a wooden box by sundown. Savvy?'

They all nodded in blind obedience.

CHAPTER TEN

The growing crowd of people that filled the street and boardwalks moved aside temporarily as the morning stagecoach made its way down the main street and was halted outside the stage depot. Dust rose up into the air as the vehicle's driver rested a boot on the brake pole and then firmly wrapped his hefty leathers around it. The dust-caked driver patted the inch-thick layer of grime off himself before turning and dragging the solitary bag off the roof.

He waited for the coach door to open and his passenger disembark. The driver lowered the canvas bag into the arms of the lean man.

'Here you go, stranger,' he quipped.

'I'm much obliged, old timer,' the passenger said as he closed the stagecoach door and then slid a cigar from his frock coat and bit off its end.

The driver descended from his high perch and looked at the well-dressed man. He had not seen anyone like Keno's top gun before and had no idea how dangerous his one and only passenger was.

'You got another one of them tobacco sticks, friend?' he asked as the man struck a match with a thumbnail and raised it to his cigar.

The eyes of the stranger looked at the driver. He pulled another of his expensive smokes from his jacket pocket and handed it to the old man.

'Here,' he muttered as his filled his own lungs with the acrid smoke and then allowed it to slowly filter through his teeth. 'Enjoy it, old timer. It's probably the most expensive cigar you've ever had.'

The smiling driver looked the visitor to Broken Lance up and down as he fumbled in his dusty coat until his fingers located a match.

'You in town on business?' he asked.

The slim gunman nodded as he sucked on the cigar as his eyes studied the busy street.

'You could say that,' he whispered.

The stagecoach driver struck a match and then lit the cigar he was chewing on. A broader smile etched his dust covered features as he leaned against the depot sign.

'My name's Charlie, friend,' he told the man. 'What they call you?'

The lean stranger looked at the old man.

'They call me Billy Montana,' he replied before pushing his coat-tails over his gun grips.

The smile vanished from old Charlie's face as the name sank into his dusty brain. He had heard the name before. He straightened up as best his age-weary frame could manage and swallowed hard.

'The same Billy Montana who resides in Waco?' he managed to ask.

Montana nodded. 'The same.'

The driver was suddenly terrified. He began to shake as he puffed nervously on the cigar. It was like staring into the eyes of death just to look at Montana.

'I'd best check in with the depot manager, Billy,' Charlie stammered as he slowly edged away from the sign towards the office doorway. 'I'll be seeing you. Thanks for the cigar.'

Montana did not utter another word. He simply turned on his boot heels and walked down boardwalk steps with his canvas bag tucked under his right arm while his right hand rested on his pearl-handled gun grip.

The driver shut the depot office door behind him and made his way to the seated manager. He pulled the cigar from his lips and panted fearfully as his mind imagined how close he had come to riling one of the most dangerous men in the territory.

The manager glanced up from his paperwork.

'What's the matter with you, Charlie?' he asked. 'You look like you just seen a ghost.'

'Do you know who I just brung to town?' the driver quaked as he tried to stop himself shaking. 'I just carried Billy Montana here from Waco. Billy Montana!'

The depot manager sat upright. His clipboard and papers slid off his knees and landed on the floor with a bump.

'Billy Montana's in town?'

Charlie sucked on the cigar. 'He sure is. I practically demanded he give me this cigar. I was lucky not to get myself shot.'

'Why's he in Broken Lance, Charlie?'

The old timer exhaled. 'I hear that there's only one reason that critter goes any place. He must be here to kill someone.'

The manager shrugged. 'You gotta admit, the town has more than enough varmints who deserve killing, Charlie.'

The driver nodded. 'I wonder who it is?'

CHAPTER ELEVEN

The busy streets of Broken Lance were perfect for anyone who did not wish to be observed too easily or shot in the back. As Jackson walked down the crowded thoroughfare amid people and animals, he did not notice the man who was watching his every movement.

Rex Carter moved carefully from one store front to the next as he carefully shadowed the tall man Pontious Longshank feared was gunning for him. The gunman had heard the shots from inside the Rattler Saloon just like everyone else in the street but he had not imagined that the high-shouldered figure he was following had been anything but a witness to whatever had occurred there.

Unlike most men who had just survived a show-down, Jackson appeared unruffled.

Carter moved through the crowd.

With every step he was getting closer to Jackson. The sheriff continued to move down the street at a casual pace as the determined gunman gained ground on his prey.

He rested a hand on his gun grip as he stepped off the boardwalk and moved between a string of saddle horses secured to a hitching rail. Carter could almost taste the bonus money he had been promised by Longshank.

His ruthless eyes squinted as he forced his way through the crowd of townsfolk. A sturdy black horse pulling a buckboard appeared directly before Carter, forcing the gunman to step aside. By the time the vehicle had passed him, Carter could not see the tall man he was trailing.

His ruthless eyes vainly searched for Jackson.

He looked to his right. The boardwalk on the corner was at least three feet higher than the ground he was stood upon. Carter pushed his way through the people who were milling around and walked up the steps on to the boardwalk.

Carter squinted as he searched for the mountainous Jackson in the crowded main street.

A cruel smile etched his unshaven face as he sighted his target. His hand dropped on to his gun. His fingers curled around the smooth grip and then curled around the trigger. Masked by the countless townsfolk, he carefully slid the gun out of its holster and rested it against his leg.

Jackson had stopped outside the livery stable across the wide street.

A bead of sweat trailed down from his leather hat-band as the gunman considered his shot. Carter moved around a porch upright in a bid to find a clear view of the tall man he intended killing. Finally, the well-paid killer found the perfect place to shoot from without being spotted by the numerous souls that filled the street.

Carter tucked himself between the porch upright and a mountainous stack of crates on the corner. His vicious eyes burned across the distance between Jackson and his lethal six-shooter. The weapon slid from the holster as his thumb pulled back on its hammer.

He was about to raise the gun when Jackson turned. Carter stared at the unexpected object on Jackson's chest. The hired gunman was startled by the sight.

Blazing sunlight glinted off the tin star like a precious diamond. It dazzled Carter. Slowly he lowered the .45 as his mind tried to work out why Keno's top gun was wearing the insignia of a lawman.

Taken aback by the sight of the sheriff's star, Rex Carter released his hammer and slid the gun back into his holster. His mind raced.

Carter tried to reason with the fact that the man Longshank had sent him to assassinate was obviously something utterly different to what he thought he was.

This man was no hired gun like himself.

Not even in Broken Lance would his breed be given the job of sheriff. Carter rubbed his whiskered face as his mind attempted to calculate his options.

It was one thing killing a stranger, but it was a whole different kettle of fish shooting a star-packer, he thought. Carter bit his lower lip.

Whoever the tall stranger was it seemed certain to Carter that he had not been sent by Keno.

His eyes burned into the broad-shouldered figure of Tim Jackson. Carter moved away from the corner as gossiping females and distracted men jostled by him.

He wondered what Longshank would want him to do once he knew the truth about the young stranger he had attempted to kill up on the hillside earlier. Then another more urgent thought filled his confused mind.

Keno's top gun might already be in town. If not, he would probably be arriving at any time.

Swiftly, Carter turned on his heels and glared at the scores of faces that kept on coming at him. He adjusted his gun-belt and then headed back to where he knew he would find Longshank.

The devilish old man had to be warned that Keno's gunman was not the tall stranger after all. Carter started to run as best he could against the tide of townsfolk.

He had to warn Longshank before it was too late, he silently told himself. As Carter jogged down the busy thoroughfare he realized that if the stubborn Longshank got shot and killed, he would never get paid his bonus money.

CHAPTER TWELVE

Jackson dried his sweating brow on his shirt sleeve and then entered the livery stable. The shadows within the tall structure felt good to the high-shouldered lawman as he paced into the heart of the shadows.

'What the hell are you doing back here, boy?'

Jackson paused, looked over his shoulder and grinned at the blacksmith.

'I need me a saddle horse, Griff,' he replied.

'What for?' Griff asked. 'Nobody with half a brain goes riding at this time of day.'

Jackson rested a hand on the wall and looked at the blacksmith. 'I'm going to take a ride up the valley.'

Griff frowned. 'Are you *loco*?'

'I must be,' Jackson shrugged. 'I take me a job as a star-packer knowing that all Hell is about to break loose. I head into the Rattler and have to kill two critters that was trying to kill me. Yep, I'm *loco*. Now have you got a horse I can hire, or not?'

The blacksmith grinned wide. 'You need a stiff drink by the sound of it, boy.'

'You might be right,' Jackson smiled.

Griff pulled a quart of whiskey from his leather apron and handed it to the lawman.

'Take a few slugs of that,' he advised.

Jackson accepted the bottle as the muscular blacksmith walked to the stalls of horses. The lawman pulled the cork and took a long swallow. The fiery liquor burned its way down into his guts.

'That's real good rye!' Jackson croaked as he rammed the cork back into the neck of the bottle. He trailed Griff to the stalls and watched as the blacksmith led a quarter horse out into the middle of the stable.

Griff held the bridle of the horse and looked at the sheriff.

'Does this 'un suit you?' he asked.

Jackson nodded. 'It ain't very tall but it looks sturdy enough, Griff.'

Griff grinned. 'I know it ain't as good as your grey but this little gelding ain't tuckered like your stallion, son.'

'Toss my saddle on it,' Jackson said as he exhaled and then turned to stare out into the bright street. 'I'm starting to get mighty tuckered myself. This heat ain't normal.'

The blacksmith placed a dry blanket on the gelding's back and patted it down. As he lifted Jackson's saddle up and onto the back of the horse he glanced at the lawman.

'It gets hotter,' he said.

Jackson raised an eyebrow. 'Hardly seems possible but I'll take your word for it.'

Griff reached under the horse's belly and grabbed the cinch strap before threading it through the metal loops. He tightened the cinch and then unhooked the fender.

'You heading to the mines?'

'Yep,' Jackson nodded. 'I'm just checking a few things out before the fat hits the skillet, Griff.'

'Who'd you kill up at the Rattler, boy?'

'Two of Ely's henchmen,' Jackson sighed.

Griff led the quarter horse across the straw-covered dirt floor and handed the reins to the tall young lawman.

'I'll get you a couple of canteens full of cold water,' he said. 'The valley gets even hotter than Broken Lance at this time of day.'

Jackson returned the bottle of whiskey to the blacksmith and then hauled his long frame up onto the back of the unfamiliar mount. A few minutes passed before he accepted the pair of cold heavy canteens from Griff.

'I can't figure out why you're still hanging around town with that target on your chest, son,' Griff sighed as he watched Jackson hang the canteens from his saddle horn. 'You oughta high-tail it while you still can.'

Jackson smiled as he gathered up the slack in the long leathers.

'There's a mighty pretty female in town I'd like to get to know, Griff,' he shrugged. 'Besides I can't leave my grey stallion here just 'coz a few folks are starting to shoot at me, can I?'

'I can't think of a better reason to leave,' Griff answered truthfully. 'A dead star-packer ain't much use to a female or a high-shouldered grey stallion.'

Jackson touched his hat brim and tapped his spurs.

'I'll keep that in mind, Griff,' he said over his wide shoulder as he allowed the quarter horse to walk out of the livery stable and out into the merciless sun.

The blacksmith watched as the tall young

lawman steered the quarter horse out into the street. He did not take his eyes off Jackson until the young star-packer had navigated his way through the crowd and disappeared from view.

Griff's shovel of a hand rubbed his wide neck anxiously.

'I hope you know what you're damn well doing, son.' Griff sighed and turned. ''Coz I sure don't.'

CHAPTER THIRTEEN

The wooden boards shook loudly under Carter's boots as he ran along the front of the building and turned into the narrow alleyway. Carter did not slow his pace until he reached his horse still tied up to the porch. He clenched his gloved fist and pounded on the door. He was about to start shouting for Longshank's bodyguard when, to his utter surprise, the door swung into the dark corridor.

Instantly, Carter knew something was wrong.

Very wrong.

In all the time he had worked for Pontious Longshank he had never known the rear door of the substantial building to be either unlocked or unguarded.

He drew a .45 and cocked its hammer.

His eyes narrowed and strained to see in the

gloom which the ancient Longshank relished exist-ing in. The hired gunman moved as quietly as his spurs would allow into the neglected structure.

With his gun moving from one shadow to the next, Carter proceeded deeper into the depths of the building to where he knew Longshank had his office.

After a dozen steps he halted.

He inhaled deeply through his flared nostrils. The aroma was one which he had never encoun-tered inside the unlit building before.

Gun smoke!

Carter looked all around him. This was the first time he had ever entered this dark place without being guided by the huge bodyguard, he thought.

'Boss?' he whispered in a vain attempt to locate Longshank. 'Are you in here?'

There was no response.

Carter gritted his teeth and began walking again. He stopped again but this time it was not his idea. Something big on the floor was blocking his path.

He knelt and reached out with his free hand. His fingers located Bruno the bodyguard. Carter rubbed his fingers together. Only blood was that sticky, he told himself as he slowly rose back up and carefully stepped over the large, lifeless body.

Two more steps and he found the office door.

The smell of gun smoke was even stronger here. Carter held his breath and turned the door handle. He pushed the door inward. Smoke hung about five feet above the floor of the office.

Carter tilted his head and stared at the desk. The light from the dirty office window highlighted the blood-splattered wall behind the empty chair.

The gunman stepped forward and looked over the desk down at the pitiful body. Longshank lay in a pool of his own gore against the wall. The bloody holes in his scrawny body told their own story. Longshank must have refused to pay the hired gunman what he owed Keno.

It was a dumb mistake. One which he had paid the ultimate price for.

Carter fumed at the sight of the lifeless corpse. He swung on his heels and looked around the office. He wondered where Longshank hid his fortune.

The gunman searched every inch of the smoke-filled room before having to admit to himself that it had not been hidden here. Carter desperately wanted his wages so that he could get out of Broken Lance as fast as possible. He was owed wages and was determined to get every last penny of them one way or another. If he happened to find Longshank's hidden fortune as well, he would take that, too.

His former employer was infamous for the fact that he did not trust or use banks. Wherever Longshank's money was, it was in cash. All he had to do was find it.

After satisfying himself that there were no hidden safe or strongbox in the office or corridor, Carter retraced his tracks back to the alleyway outside and emerged from the rear of the large edifice.

His mind raced.

He pulled his reins free, grabbed his saddle horn and stepped into his stirrup. Carter threw his right leg over the cantle and steadied himself upon the saddle. His eyes looked around the squalid alley for any sign of the person who had just slain his boss and Bruno.

But whoever had killed them was long gone.

It seemed obvious that Keno's top gun must have failed to recoup the money Longshank owed his employer. Otherwise the old man and Bruno might still be alive, Carter thought.

He turned his animal.

Someone in Broken Lance knew where Longshank lived, Carter told himself. All he had to do was find out where and pay him a visit. Carter knew that his best chance of locating the miser's fortune was to start there.

He whipped his mount sharply with his reins. The animal started back toward the main street. As the horse trotted along the confines of the alley, Carter reasoned that it might be days before anyone discovered the bodies. Eventually, it would be the smell of decaying flesh that would alert folks to the gruesome deeds within the building's dark corridors.

As Carter's mount rounded the corner the gunman felt the hair on the nape of his neck rise. Suddenly he realized that Keno's henchman had to be still in town.

As he rode through the busy street Carter wondered if the unknown assassin might be watching him. His eyes darted around the hundreds of faces below his high perch, knowing one of them could belong to the killer.

A killer who was probably still determined to find Longshank's hidden money as badly as he was.

Carter gripped his reins as he navigated a safe

route through the crowded street in search of the ancient old miser's home. Was Keno's top gun watching? What if he was following?

He nervously glanced over his shoulder as the gelding continued down the street. As he aimed the nose of his horse he wondered if the unknown gunman might know where Longshank lived. At least it was a good place to start.

The morning sun was hotter than the bowels of Hell but a cold shiver defiantly traced Carter's spine as he drew rein outside the offices of *The Gazette*.

Carter dismounted and looped his leathers around the newspaper's hitching rail. As he stepped up and entered the office, standing on a hotel balcony from way across the street Billy Montana struck a match and lit a cigar.

From his lofty vantage point, the deadly observer had an uninterrupted view of the entire main street. Smoke trailed from his mouth as he calmly descended the steps down to the street and stood beside the mount he had hired only moments earlier.

The smiling Montana rested a shoulder against the horse and waited for Carter to re-emerge from the newspaper office.

CHAPTER FOURTEEN

The putrid smell of death still lingered in the Rattler as the undertaker and his assistant dutifully carried the crudely constructed coffin through the saloon's swing doors and out into the hot street. Both bodies had been carted off to the funeral parlour, but the unwelcome scent of their rotting flesh remained on the staircase and floor of the saloon. The baking hot saloon already had several conflicting aromas within its four square walls. Death had only added one more sickening fragrance to the others. Joe Lever had attempted to mask the odious smell with handfuls of fresh sawdust but all the bartender had achieved was to add to the aroma.

Men lit their pipes and cigars around the horse-shoe counter so they might continue drinking with only the smell of tobacco smoke filling their nostrils.

It was a vain exercise. Nothing could disguise the truth, no matter how much sawdust buried it beneath. The regular patrons of the Rattler had remained long after the gun smoke had gone. They continued drinking under their clouds of tobacco smoke as the sound of horsemen echoed off the walls of the saloon.

Drunken eyes glanced briefly from their glasses at the riders dragging their long leathers to stop their mounts outside the Rattler. The sound of spurs stepping up onto the boardwalk filled the saloon before the devilish killers entered.

The swing doors rocked feverishly on their hinges as one after another, the men entered. There was a strange look carved into each of their faces.

It was the look of failure.

Buren Ely's small army of venomous back-shooters had returned empty-handed to the Rattler from every corner of the sprawling settlement and marched through the saloon to the bar. They had not managed to find the tall young sheriff and were angry and fearful in equal portions.

Angry that they had not been able to avenge their dead cohorts.

Fearful of the wrath they knew Ely would surely unleash upon them for failing to obey his orders.

The paying customers spread out across the saloon as Ely's killers rested against the bar counter. They beat their fists on the damp counter top. Joe Lever did not have to be told what the ruthless men desired. He rushed forward with a bottle of whiskey and started to ply them with the hard liquor. The hired gunmen snorted as they looked down into their glasses

The fiery whiskey had barely had time to burn their throats on its way to their gullets when they heard the screaming coming from the corridor up on the landing.

As Lever refilled their glasses the men cast their attention to the irate yelling which was growing louder with each passing heartbeat.

The gunmen had hired their dubious skills to many men over the years but none of their previous bosses could hold a candle to the unpredictable Buren Ely. There was something about the man which made even the most lethal of them quake in fear of his wrath.

The screaming was not coming from Ely's lungs though. The screaming belonged to one of the many drugged females he filled the Rattler with.

Ely knew how to obtain vast supplies of laudanum from his numerous shady contacts and plied the females with the drug until they were totally addicted.

The gunmen looked up at the landing as Ely marched to the top of the staircase with a near naked female in his grip. The girl was being held by her mane of long, red hair and was being shaken violently. Ely wore only his long johns with his gun-belt strapped around his middle. It was a hideous and amusing sight but not one living soul dared to say a thing to the snarling saloon owner.

Ely stopped when he spied his henchmen and diverted his anger in their direction.

Pointing down into the belly of the saloon, Ely glared down at his men.

'Did you kill him?' he shouted. 'Did you kill that snot-nosed bastard like I told you?'

The hired gunmen answered his question with their mutual silence. Every one of the heavily armed gang kept their eyes focused on their glasses as the bartender refilled them once more.

'You didn't kill him?' Ely raged. 'Hell, he's so big even the worst of you couldn't miss his sorrowful carcass.'

The gunman closest to the staircase swallowed

his whiskey, gritted his teeth and then turned and looked up at his fuming boss.

'Wherever that varmint is, he sure ain't in Broken Lance, boss,' Tom Brody said firmly. 'We searched every corner of town and the big galoot just can't be found.'

Ely rubbed his face as he held the female like a rag doll.

'He just has to be in town,' he snorted before considering the statement more carefully for a few seconds. 'But if he has high-tailed it out of Broken Lance that might be just perfect, boys.'

'Let me go, Buren,' the red-haired girl whimpered.

Ely looked down at the pitiful creature. His bloodshot eyes moved over her nakedness with little more interest than he would show a stray dog.

He returned his attention to his men below him.

'Get up here!' Ely growled at them loudly. 'Every damn one of you.'

The gunmen downed their drinks and then reluctantly turned and did as they were told. Ely pushed the female aside and shook his fist at her. The half-dazed girl swayed and watched the brutal Ely walk toward his private rooms.

'Get earning, gal!' he ordered her with a shout.

The female waited for the line of gunmen to reach the landing and trail Ely back to his private quarters before she started down towards the paying customers.

She pulled at her torn blouse in an attempt to cover up her modesty. Six months earlier, before she had ever met Ely, the red-headed female would never have allowed herself to be seen by anyone in this condition.

That had been before she had tasted the evil beverage Ely had plied her with. Then she had become just like all the rest of the unfortunate females in the Rattler.

Now all she could think about was making enough money to give to Ely so that he would give her the drink which dulled her senses and did not allow her to see the truth.

CHAPTER FIFTEEN

Tim Jackson sat uncomfortably on the quarter horse as the short-legged animal continued to canter down the valley toward the place he had been told the gold mines and the warehouse were situated. The lawman looked this way and that at the countless abandoned mines that had been dug out in the once pristine hills. Whatever natural life there had been in the blisteringly hot valley was now long gone. A scattering of trees were all that remained.

The prospectors had been thorough, he thought.

Jackson removed his hat and shook the sweat from it before mopping his brow and then replacing the Stetson. He kept tapping his spurs to encourage the horse on.

He had thought that Broken Lance was hot, but

now as the horse rode deeper and deeper into the valley, he realized this place was even hotter.

A shimmering heat haze obscured his view of what lay before him. It was like trying to see through a constantly moving waterfall. The burning air danced before him while the blazing sun burned through his trail gear.

The valley was painful.

Jackson was about to haul rein and turn back when he heard something far ahead. The lawman leaned over the neck of his quarter horse and narrowed his eyes.

As the horse continued to obey his spurs, Jackson slowly began to see something in the bright rays of the merciless sun.

Slowly, reluctantly, broken images began to fit together.

As the horse beneath his saddle drew closer to the shattered jigsaw he knew that he had finally reached the warehouse. He dried his eyes as he passed a handful of wooden cabins and three times as many tents. Men were going about their business as the horse neared the well-constructed structure he had been told housed the bars of gold.

Jackson pulled his leathers to his chest. The horse stopped. He could see and hear the smelter just beyond the warehouse.

Smoke rose up into the sky from the smelter's chimney.

Jackson went to dismount when he heard the sound of half a dozen rifles being cocked and readied for action. The tall rider glanced around him.

Guards had their Winchesters trained on him.

'Who are you, stranger?' a voice called out from behind him. 'Answer quick or die even quicker.'

'I'm the new sheriff,' Jackson replied as he slowly raised his arms to reveal his hands were empty. 'My name's Jackson. The mayor told me about you fellas.'

The men closed in on their target.

'Throw a leg over the neck of that horse and slide down.' The voice ordered. 'Make it quick.'

Jackson did as he was told.

He looped a leg over the head of the quarter horse and then slid the short distance to the ground. His eyes darted between the guards as they kept their distance with their guns aimed at him.

'He's wearing a star, Zack,' one of the guards shouted to the owner of the deep voice behind Jackson.

'A lotta men wear stars,' drawled Zack Collins, the foreman of the gold mines, as he came into view. 'It don't always follow that they're lawmen.'

Jackson kept his hands high as he turned his tall frame and looked at Collins head on.

'I'm a lawman OK, friend,' he said. 'Kinda wishing I was something else right about now, though.'

A smile lit up Collins' face as he lowered the rifle. The man who looked about twice Jackson's age studied the tall figure. He looked impressed.

'Where in tarnation did Healy find you, Jackson?' Collins smiled. 'I ain't never met anyone as tall as you are.'

Jackson waited until the rest of the watchful guards had also lowered their rifles before he brought his hands down. He looked at Collins.

'Seems like there's trouble brewing in town and the mayor wants me to kinda stop it, Zack,' Jackson muttered as he stood like a lofty pine in a sea of sand. 'I figure he's got more faith in me than I have. Seems like a certain Buren Ely has been having his henchmen kill every star-packer that the mayor has hired lately. I had to kill two of them earlier when they tried to add me to their tally.'

Collins looked impressed. 'You killed two of Ely's cut-throats?'

Jackson nodded. 'I had to. They was shooting at me.'

Collins smiled. 'My name's Zack Collins, Sheriff. I'm the foreman around here. I ain't sure how lucky you'll be in stopping them varmints from trying to steal this gold before we can get it to the mint, but me and the boys could sure use the help of someone who knows how to handle his six-shooters.'

Jackson nodded. 'The mayor said that you were going to transport it yourselves. Is that right?'

Collins nodded. 'Yep, it sure is.'

'Mighty risky, if you ask me,' the sheriff said. 'It's a long way to the mint.'

'An awful long way,' Collins agreed.

'But there must be a thousand places for them varmints to bushwhack your boys between here and Austin. A thousand places for them to get their hands on them gold bricks, friend,' Jackson reasoned. 'That's real risky if you ask me.'

The foreman of the mining operation started to walk and the tall lawman followed. Collins looked up at Jackson. He was still grinning.

'It's not as risky as it sounds, Jackson,' he started

to explain as they headed beyond the well-guarded warehouse. 'You see, I intend taking the wagon we've bin adapting only as far as the railroad spur.'

Jackson looked down at Collins. 'What railroad spur?'

'The one the railroad company branched off from the main tracks,' Collins explained. 'It's only operational when the ranchers got a couple of thousand steers to ship east.'

Jackson nodded. 'So you intend putting all them gold bricks in the baggage car?'

The older man shook his head. 'Nope. I've made arrangements for the entire wagon to be placed on a flatbed car. The gold will never leave the wagon. I'm sending six guards to protect it all the way to Austin.'

'How are you going to get a hefty wagon up and on to a train flatbed?' the youngster asked. 'The thing will weigh a ton or more when it's loaded.'

'The railroad's supplying the strongest crane they got to do the job fast and easy, Jackson,' grinned Collins. 'I just got news that the crane is at the spur already. All we gotta do is transport our cargo there. Then it'll travel non-stop to the mint.'

The high-shouldered sheriff nodded. 'You seem to have figured it all out, Collins.'

'Apart from getting the wagon to the spur safely,' Collins differed. 'That's the main weakness in my plan.'

Jackson sighed. 'How far is it to the railroad spur from here?'

'Exactly twenty-three miles,' Collins replied as he led Jackson between a maze of shacks and sheds. 'Twenty-three damn dangerous miles where them scum-suckers can dry-gulch us in a dozen perfect places. The terrain around here looks like it was designed by a bushwhacker. I ain't gonna get too much rest until we see the wagon secured to that damn locomotive, son.'

Jackson was thoughtful. 'The journey to the railroad spur is the most vulnerable, OK? The one advantage you've got is that they don't know when you'll be leaving.'

'They must have someone watching and waiting for us to set out, son,' Collins guessed. 'When that galoot see's us heading away from here, he'll ride into Broken Lance and bring the whole bunch of vermin down on us.'

Jackson rubbed his chin. 'I'll ride the hills when I leave here and find Ely's spy. When I get my hands on him, he ain't gonna be tellin' nobody a darn thing.'

Collins laughed and slapped the muscular arm of the tall sheriff. Both turned a corner and stopped. Collins gestured at the wagon. Three men were hammering iron rivets into its reinforced body.

'What do you think of that?' he asked.

'That's mighty impressive, Zack,' Jackson smiled.

Jackson wandered toward the wagon. The entire body of the prairie schooner had been encased in metal plates.

'Well?' Collins asked proudly.

'Like I said, it's impressive,' Jackson repeated.

Collins inhaled like a proud parent. 'We've reinforced the axle and wheels. We've even designed side plates to protect the eight-horse team from getting shot.'

Jackson nodded as he observed the enclosed driver's seat.

'Looks like you've thought of about everything,' he noted.

Collins was about to speak when he heard and saw a rider thundering toward them. The guards let him through their protective lines.

Collins rested his knuckles on his hips as the horseman drew rein and leapt from his lathered-up mount. He ran the short distance to the foreman and nodded.

'I told them,' the exhausted rider gasped.

Collins nodded. 'Good. Now get that horse under cover and wash him down.'

Curious, Tim Jackson watched as the foreman stared off into the heat haze. He approached and looked down at the thoughtful face until Collins turned to face him.

'What was that all about?' the sheriff wondered.

'I had one of my boys inform the mayor and his partners at the Cattleman Club that we're headed out at midnight,' Collins said.

'I figured you were trying to keep that a secret,' Jackson said. 'How come you sent one of your men to spill the beans?'

'They're major shareholders in this company, Jackson,' Collins sighed. 'I had to tell them.'

Jackson mopped the sweat off his brow. 'I'm headed back to town via the hills, Collins. If I find anyone spying on you and your boys I'll deal with it.'

Both men made their way back to the quarter horse. Collins stopped as Jackson mounted the sturdy animal. Jackson glanced over his wide shoulder at the foreman.

'I'll be looking out for you at midnight,' he

vowed and touched his hat brim.

Collins watched as the young lawman spurred and rode back toward the distant town. The foreman turned on his boots and strode back to where his men were finishing their conversion of the wagon.

For the first time in quite a while Collins was impressed with Healy's selection of the new sheriff. This one looked as though he might just live a few days.

For the better part of an hour Jackson had guided the short-legged saddle horse up the crumbling rocks until it finally reached the top of the valley. The horseman eased back on his long leathers and stared out across the sun-drenched terrain as they rolled all the way back to Broken Lance.

The lawman held the quarter horse in check as his eyes tried to focus on both sides of the void. He could not make out anything of danger on the opposite side of the valley but as his muscular neck returned to what lay ahead of him he caught a brief glimpse of something about a half mile ahead of him.

Jackson stepped down from his saddle and placed his hat on the ground before the exhausted horse. Without taking his eyes off the intriguing object ahead of him, he filled the bowl of his upturned Stetson with water from one of his canteens.

The horse drank quickly as the lawman hung the canteen back on the saddle horn. He lifted his Stetson off the baked surface of the ground and placed it on his head. The remnants of water droplets trickled down his face and neck as he pulled his carbine from the scabbard and cocked its mechanism.

A spent casing flew from the magazine as Jackson rested the Winchester's long barrel on the brow of his saddle. He closed one eye and stared through the rifle sights at the distant object.

As he aimed the weapon it became obvious that what he was looking at was a man hidden in the rocks. A man with a rifle just like his own.

The lawman bit his lip and then eased back on his rifle trigger. The deafening shot made the tired horse jolt as Jackson swiftly jerked the hand guard down and back up.

'Easy, boy!' Jackson whispered to the skittish mount.

Jackson watched the hidden figure move away from the edge of the rocky hillside and find better cover. He breathed slow and easy as he waited to see what the other man would do.

He did not have to wait long.

The rifle bullet came hurtling from the rocks at him a split second before he heard the sound of the Winchester being fired. To his surprise the shot took his hat off his head, sending the Stetson cartwheeling down into the chasm.

'Damn you!' Jackson cursed. 'That was my best hat.'

The sheriff tucked the wooden stock into his shoulder and then fired back. He saw dust rise into the cloudless blue sky before he readied the rifle again.

Jackson fired again.

The noise made by the stricken bushwhacker as his shot ripped into him filled the lawman's ears. Without a moment's hesitation, Jackson looped his reins around his wrist and mounted the nervous horse.

He rode across the cracked sun-baked surface of the hillside at pace towards where he had last spotted his adversary's gun smoke.

Jackson pulled back on his leathers, looped his long right leg over the gelding's head and slid the short distance to the ground.

He cocked the rifle again and cautiously approached the rocks. Fresh blood covered the top of the rocks where the gunman had been hiding.

Jackson clutched the repeating rifle in his hands and stepped up onto the rocks. His long legs made short work of the obstacle.

Then a blinding cloud of gun smoke erupted from behind the sand-coloured rocks. Jackson felt the heat of the bullet as it passed close to his neck muscles.

Like all creatures fighting for their very lives, Jackson immediately readied his Winchester. He pulled on the trigger and clenched his teeth as the deafening sound of the rifle spewing lead filled his already ringing ears.

The high-shouldered sheriff saw the plumes of blinding fury erupt below him as hot lead cut through the dense smoke.

He fired into the smoke and automatically jerked his rifle's mechanism again. Jackson staggered on the rocks as he realized that the volley of bullets had torn through his shirt and ripped across his ribs. Then it fell silent. He waited for the gun smoke to clear. When it did, he knew why the shooting had stopped so abruptly.

His eyes stared down at the dead gunman.

Blood covered what was left of the bushwhacker and trickled down the rocks in sickening streams towards the rim of the rocks.

Satisfied that this brief fight was over, Jackson turned and then jumped back down to where the wide-eyed quarter horse stood. The wounded lawman snatched up his reins off the ground and grabbed hold of his saddle horn. His eyes glanced down on the torn fabric of his shirt and the scarlet stain which covered it.

'I oughta tell the mayor I want a pay rise,' he muttered as he lifted his leg and poked it into the stirrup. Using his powerful arms he hauled himself up onto the back of the gelding. 'This is even more dangerous than busting broncos.'

He slid the smoking Winchester into its scabbard and raised his hand against the merciless rays of the sun. The skin on his face was beginning to burn.

'If I live long enough I'm gonna buy me a new hat,' he sighed before looking down at the sprawling settlement below his high vantage point. He wondered how a town that looked so peaceful could be so troublesome.

As Jackson gathered up his reins he felt something trace a trail down his temple from his hair.

He lifted the tails of his bandana and wiped his wet brow.

Only then did he notice the bandana was stained with crimson gore. He raised his fingers and found the graze on the crown of his head. It was deep and meant that one of the gunman's bullets had come close to snuffing out his young candle.

Mighty close.

Jackson stared at the dead body.

'It's a good job I ain't no taller, friend,' he told the corpse. 'You'd have split my head in two otherwise.'

The lawman tapped his spurs and continued across the roof of the valley towards the sun-bleached settlement. There was a growing anger in the young sheriff as the quarter horse obeyed its temporary master.

Jackson was angry at the trouble Buren Ely and his band of lethal gunmen were creating in what would otherwise be a quiet and peaceful town. He was also angry at himself for getting hopelessly entangled in its problems.

But being the kind of man he was, Jackson knew that he was in far too deep to do anything except play the hand that fate had dealt him.

No matter what it might cost him, Jackson would see this through to the very end.

The star-packer tapped his spurs and continued on down toward the distant town. The young lawman was getting angrier with every stride of his mounts thundering hoofs.

His injuries were hurting bad.

Real bad.

CHAPTER SIXTEEN

The offices of *The Gazette* seemed to know where every living soul within the town's unmarked borders lived. Rex Carter had learned where Pontious Longshank had owned a small house before his sudden demise. The gunman was riding from the newspaper office to the furthest part of Broken Lance to find it. The further he rode away from the centre of town, the thinner the crowd was until Carter found himself travelling along empty streets.

Carter knew that Longshank had never trusted banks and since arriving in Broken Lance the miser had horded his small fortune in hard cash. The gunman felt sure that it was hidden inside the house and if he was right, he was going to take it all.

As the excited gunman whipped the tail of

his mount with his loose leathers and drove on to where he had been informed he would locate Longshank's home, he had totally forgotten that he was not the only gunman in search of the old man's money.

Billy Montana was also keen to find the fortune that the old miser had stolen from his employer. The mysterious man known only as Keno had served time for the money that his partner had fled to Broken Lance with.

Keno wanted the money and knew that Montana would get it no matter how much blood had to be spilled in the gruesome venture. Montana had been patient and was trailing Carter at a safe distance along the quiet outskirts of town.

His notion was that if you don't know where you're going, follow someone who does.

The seasoned hired killer kept Carter in sight as he followed him through the winding empty streets to the very edge of town.

The house that Carter was headed towards was a weathered structure which looked as if it were about to topple off its foundations at any time. There were no other dwellings within a half mile of the house and it did not even look as if anyone had ever lived there. But the deadly Montana reasoned that it was exactly the sort of place he might expect Longshank to live in.

Montana drew rein and eased his rented mount into the cover of untended bushes. He pulled down on some branches and glared through the gap at Carter as the horseman approached the squalid house. His cruel eyes watched as Carter stopped his horse and dismounted beside a broken fence.

He sighed in amusement as Carter crossed the front yard and then forced his way into the ramshackle house. It had not required too much effort for the door to be separated from its hinges.

Calmly, Montana stepped down from the horse and tied its reins to the bushes which hid it from sight. The ruthless Montana then started to approach the house.

Most men of his profession might have shown caution when closing the distance between themselves and an unknown gunman, but not Montana. He walked straight across the dusty trail in defiance of Carter's ability with his guns.

The well-dressed killer could hear the sound of Carter as he frantically searched for his dead employer's hidden money. As Montana pushed the gate open he listened to the frenzied noises coming from within the small dwelling.

Carter was far too busy to even notice the ominous figure that was within striking distance of him.

Montana walked to the side of the front yard and sat down upon an upturned barrel. He withdrew a cigar from his case and then bit the tip of the cigar off and spat it away.

He patiently slid the silver case back into his coat pocket and then withdrew a match.

Montana struck a match with his thumbnail and lit the fine Havana. The experienced Montana knew that it was pointless getting involved in the search.

He would let Longshank's employee do all the dirty work for him. Montana savoured the taste of the fine cigar between his teeth and calmly listened to the fevered sounds of searching coming from inside the small house.

Montana instinctively checked both his holstered .45s as he waited for Carter to exit the neglected property. He returned the gleaming guns back into their hand-tooled holsters and then removed the cigar from his lips and tapped the ash onto the dusty ground. He returned the cigar to his mouth and watched the open doorway like a puma waiting for its chosen prey to re-emerge into the blazing midday sun.

Suddenly the dust-caked Rex Carter staggered out of the small dwelling, triumphantly carrying two swollen saddlebags.

Carter had barely taken three long steps when he heard laughter cut across the quiet yard. The surprised gunman stopped and turned on his heels to stare at the elegant man with the expensive cigar gripped between his teeth.

A cold shudder enveloped Carter as he released his grip on the hefty leather satchel. It dropped to the ground at his feet.

'Looks like you found it,' Montana said as he stood. 'Now all you gotta do is look scared and run.'

Carter faced the elegant man and watched as Montana pushed the tails of his frock coat over his holstered gun grips and tilted his head. Montana narrowed his icy stare and glared at the startled Carter.

'Who in tarnation are you?' Carter asked as his thumbs pushed his coat over the guns.

'I'm the man that's looking to add another notch to my gun grip, friend,' Montana answered coldly. 'Do you want to be that notch?'

Carter's mind raced as he suddenly remembered that he was not the only one looking for Longshank's hidden treasure. He swallowed hard as his face twitched.

'Are you Keno's top gun?' Carter asked feebly. He found it hard to imagine that anyone who looked so neat could possibly be a hired killer.

Montana pulled the cigar from his mouth and placed it on the barrel. He then flexed his fingers and grinned at the confused Carter.

'I imagine I must be, stranger,' he replied dryly and then pointed at the saddlebags. 'I work for Keno and he figures on sharing that loot with me.'

Carter did not believe that this cold-blooded killer would allow him to just turn-tail and run away. There was something in the face of the unflinching gunman which told Carter that whatever he did he would either have to fight or just get executed.

Reluctantly Carter squared up to Montana. 'Who the hell are you?'

'I'm Billy Montana,' the gunman calmly replied. 'I'm sure you've heard tell of me.'

Carter flexed his fingers. The name was infamous in this part of the West. Montana was known as a man who killed without mercy.

'I've heard of you,' Carter gave a nod.

Montana smiled. 'Then leave that money and high-tail it out of here while you still can. Otherwise you'll surely join Longshank in the bowels of Hell.'

'I ain't gonna leave this money,' Carter defiantly growled. 'I found this loot. It's mine and I sure ain't lettin' no fancy dude take it from me, Billy Montana.'

Montana stopped smiling.

'Then prepare to die,' he said.

'You're bluffing,' snarled Carter. 'How do I even know you *are* Billy Montana?'

There was a cold lingering silence as Keno's top gun eyed the dishevelled Carter. He raised both his hands until they hovered over his guns.

Carter was getting more and more nervous.

'For all I know you're just a fancy dude trying to bluff this pot with a pair of deuces,' he stammered.

Montana smiled. It was not the smile of a man with a sense of humour, but rather the cold smile of a deadly creature ready to kill with brutish disregard.

'There's only one way I can prove that I am who I say I am, friend,' said Montana.

Sweat poured down the spine of the hapless

Carter. He could feel his shirt clinging to his back.

'How'd you figure on doing that?' he croaked.

'Like this,' Montana answered.

Faster than Carter had ever seen anyone draw a gun from its holster, Montana whipped both weapons out of their leather pouches and fired.

It would be the last thing Rex Carter would ever see.

Montana did not stop shooting until he had expelled every bullet from his .45s and filled Longshank's hired gun with them. Carter staggered as the bullets impacted into his chest. He staggered and then slowly crumpled before falling to his knees. His eyes rolled up until the pupils disappeared under his eyelids. With blood pouring from every hole in his chest, he crashed on to his face.

Within seconds the lifeless body was encircled by a pool of crimson gore.

The deadly Montana returned his cigar to his mouth and shook the spent casings from his smoking guns as he strode toward his latest victim. He swiftly refilled the hot chambers with bullets from his belt. Montana looked around the quiet area.

When satisfied that there was not a solitary

witness to his handiwork, he holstered his guns and scooped the saddlebags off the ground.

Montana touched his hat brim to his dead opponent.

'Nice doing business with you, mister.' He smiled before heading back to his rented horse with the hefty bags hanging from his left hand. 'Shame that you thought you were a gunfighter 'coz you surely weren't.'

Montana tossed the saddlebags over the neck of his rented horse and then mounted the animal. He tapped the ash from his cigar and glanced back at the dead Carter.

He chuckled again and spurred.

CHAPTER SEVENTEEN

The Rattler grew busier as the afternoon grew older. The bar was filled with more than fifty of its regular customers. They played cards and drank heavily as eight of Ely's men shared a bottle of whiskey at the foot of the staircase and awaited instructions. Yet not all of the regular patrons of the Rattler wanted just hard liquor to quench their urges. A few of the local townsfolk wanted more to satisfy their lustful cravings.

Whilst many just wanted the brief enjoyment of female company, a small handful desired more. They wanted something that their age denied them but their wealth could purchase anyway.

This small select group of men had an arrangement with Ely and he saw to it that their carnal desire for female company was always discreetly satisfied. The wooden steps in the alley at the side of the saloon were their stairway to temporary happiness. Yet, as with everything Buren Ely did, there was an ulterior motive to his seemingly kind actions and it was about to pay dividends.

The saloon keeper had already dosed his soiled doves with enough booze and laudanum to do whatever the high-paying men wanted. With the promise of even more, the females would do exactly as Ely demanded.

Buren Ely walked to the landing, looked down into his saloon and signalled to Tom Brody. The vicious killer stood up and then climbed the stairs to where Ely waited.

'What's wrong, boss?' Brody asked.

The depraved Ely grinned and then nodded for Brody to follow. The two men strode down the corridor past half a dozen doors until they reached the saloon owner's private quarters.

They entered the room and moved across the bedroom to where the half-conscious female still lay clutching her bottle to her bosom.

Ely sat on the edge of the mattress and grabbed the female by her hair. He dragged her up into a sitting position and then looked into her half-closed eyes.

'Wake up, Katie,' Ely growled as he shook her by

the neck until her eyes cleared. 'It's time for you to go to work like we talked about.'

She frowned. 'Is he here?'

'He's here and he's waiting for you, Katie,' Ely said as he hauled her across the sheets until she was sat on the edge of the bed. Ely grabbed a bottle of perfume and rubbed her flesh with its fragrant contents until the stale smell of sweat and other bodily fluids were masked. 'I've got a couple of gals in there with him, but he really wants you.'

She smiled. 'What am I supposed to do again?'

Ely shook her violently and then pushed a small bottle of smelling salts under her nose. The strong whiff of ammonia brought her out of her daze swiftly.

'Listen, Katie,' he snarled before pulling a quart of whiskey from inside his shirt. 'You have to give him this special drink and then ask him when they're moving the gold, gal. Do you understand me?'

Blinking wildly, Katie nodded and stood.

The naked female swayed as both Brody and Ely covered her flesh in a silk robe and tied its sash around her middle. She clutched the bottle as the saloon owner led her across the room to a secret door.

'Don't you go drinking any of this,' Ely insisted. 'This is for that galoot. It's doctored. I want him to drink every damn drop so that he'll tell you everything we need to know.'

'I know,' Katie sniffed before toying with her hair. 'When I get through with him he'll tell us anything you wanna know.'

Ely hauled her across the room.

'Now go in there and get that old fool to tell you when they're moving the gold, Katie,' Ely insisted as he opened the door. 'Savvy?'

She nodded and patted the whiskey bottle cradled in the crook of her arm. 'I'll give him plenty of this baby and he'll sing like a nightingale.'

Buren Ely pushed her into the room. He closed the door and looked at Brody.

'Get in the hollow wall and listen to what old Quentin Vale has to say, Tom,' Ely ordered. 'Find out when them miners are gonna move that wagon out of the valley.'

'OK, boss.' Brody grinned and slid into the cavity between the outer wall and the specially altered bedroom. From there he could see and hear everything.

After thirty minutes Brody made his way out of the cavity and looked ashen-faced.

Ely got up from the bed and grabbed the gunman by the shoulders.

'Well?' he growled.

At that exact same moment the secret door re-opened.

Buren Ely's head looked from one to the other.

'Well? What did he say?' the saloon keeper snarled.

'The wagon is set to head out from the valley around midnight, boss,' Brody answered as he glanced across at the near-naked Katie as she walked barefoot to the bed.

Ely smiled and slapped his hands together. Then he noticed that both the female and Brody still looked confused. He stopped celebrating and grabbed Katie's mane of hair.

'What the Hell's wrong?' he shouted into her ear.

Her stained face looked at Ely. 'The bastard's dead.'

Ely released his grip and looked at Brody. 'What's she talking about, Tom?'

Brody shrugged and exhaled. 'Katie and the girls sure worked hard in there, boss. They filled Vale with that liquor you give her and then the varmint spilled the beans about the shipment.

Trouble was Katie was milking more than just information from that old critter. He up and died.'

'It weren't my fault,' Katie slurred. 'He just couldn't handle three gals at once.'

Ely stood in the centre of the room thoughtfully. After a few moments he raised his eyebrows and chuckled.

'Least ways we learned that the shipment's heading out tonight,' he mused before pointing at Brody. 'Round up the rest of the boys and head on out. You'll have plenty of time to bushwhack that wagon.'

Brody stepped up to Ely and pointed to the open doorway.

'What'll we do with that dead carcass, boss?' Brody asked. 'We can't leave it in there. It's too damn hot to leave dead critters lying around.'

'Don't fret none, Tom.' Ely grinned as he moved behind the female and slid his hands down her shoulders and cupped her breasts. 'I'll throw old Vale out of the window at sundown.'

Katie swung around. 'You're gonna do what?'

Ely grabbed her face and squeezed her cheeks until her eyes bulged.

'Shut the hell up!' he snarled. '*You* killed him.'

CHAPTER EIGHTEEN

Jackson had only just ridden into the livery stable when the sound of thundering hoofs echoed around the tall edifice. The young lawman swung around on his saddle as Brody led the rest of Ely's henchmen galloping past. Jackson dismounted and watched as the riders rode for the outskirts of town as the blacksmith walked to his side and looked him up and down.

'I warned you, Tim boy,' Griff muttered as he studied the blood-covered sheriff and sighed. 'What happened?'

'I tangled with one of Ely's boys above the valley,' Jackson answered as he walked to the forge and sat down next to the glowing coals. 'The *hombre* was perched up on top of the rocks overlooking the trail in and out from the mine. We had us a disagreement and swapped lead.'

Griff led the quarter horse to the stalls and started to remove its saddle.

'Who won?' the older man smirked.

Jackson held his hand against his side and glared at Griff as he pulled the saddle off the horse's back and draped it over one of the stalls.

'How bad do I look, Griff?'

The blacksmith pushed the horse into the stall and then made his way back to the wounded lawman. He looked down upon the sheriff and sighed heavily.

'You look plumb pitiful,' he admitted honestly.

Jackson leaned back against the bricks of the forge. 'I can't look as bad as I feel. I feel like I've bin stung by a hundred ornery hornets.'

'You look like you need a drink,' Griff said.

'I don't reckon I'll be heading back to the Rattler just yet, old timer,' Jackson joked. 'I need me doctoring.'

'The doc left town two days ago,' Griff announced. 'He won't be back for maybe a week or more.'

Jackson stood and pulled his bloody shirt away from his grazed ribs. The ripped fabric was still sticky.

'I need me a place to get patched up, Griff,'

Jackson said wearily. 'A place where I can get me some shut-eye for a few hours.'

Griff walked to the tall barn doors and stared across the street. He then turned his head and indicated for the youngster to join him.

Jackson strode to the side of the blacksmith and rested an elbow on his friend's shoulder. 'What are you looking at?'

Griff raised his big hand and pointed at the café.

'Peggy will be more than happy to patch you up, son,' he said. 'She ain't no friend of Buren Ely's, and that's for sure.'

Jackson took a step away from the blacksmith and looked over the heads of the people who were still roaming the street. The high-shouldered lawman then looked over his shoulder at Griff again.

'You reckon that she'd be willing to fix me up, Griff?' he asked. 'I don't want to scare her looking like this.'

'That little lady has seen a lot worse, boy,' Griff sighed. 'Her poor husband was killed by that pack of coyotes and he looked a whole lot worse than you do.'

Jackson rubbed his flat stomach.

'If she refuses I'll have myself a slice of pie,' he grinned.

Griff watched as the tall lawman made his way across the wide street to the small café. A sense of envy swept over the blacksmith as he recalled a time when he too once had the ability to turn a female head. He chuckled under his breath and then turned on his heels and made his way back into the depths of the stable.

The high-shouldered figure with the tin star hanging from his torn shirt stepped up onto the boardwalk outside the café and approached its door. With the sunlight filling the aromatic building he stared through the glass windowpanes at the empty chairs and tables. Jackson reached down, grabbed the door handle and entered. He closed the door behind him and stood like a statue until the handsome female emerged from the back room.

The lawman wiped the blood from his face and sheepishly glanced across the café at her.

Peggy Smith stopped in her tracks when her beautiful eyes caught sight of her latest customer.

'My God!' she gasped in horror. 'What happened to you?'

'I got too close to an *hombre* trying to kill me, I guess,' Jackson said. 'He was waiting to bushwhack somebody.'

Peggy could not conceal her concern. 'It looks like it was you, Tim.'

Jackson looked almost apologetic. 'I'm sorry to disturb you, Peg. Griff over in the livery told me that you might be willing to patch me up. I understand if you'd rather not.'

She crossed the floor and bolted the door before pulling down the blind and then turning to the tall man.

'Of course I'll tend to your wounds, Tim,' Peggy said before gently ushering him toward the rear of the café. 'This way.'

Jackson looked down at the female in surprise.

'Where we going?' he asked as they proceeded through the kitchen and entered a room which the sheriff took to be her parlour.

She pointed at a hardback chair next to a lace-covered window. 'Sit down.'

Jackson did as she instructed. Her soft hands carefully took hold of his head and gently pulled it towards her. Her handsome eyes studied the bullet graze on his bloody scalp.

'I'll clean up this head wound and then see to

the grazes on your side.' There was concern in her voice as her small hands gently tilted his head toward her.

Jackson inhaled the scent of the female and swallowed hard. The young, tall lawman had never before been in a situation like this. His large hands gripped his knees as she stood beside him and studied his still bleeding scalp.

'Thank you kindly, Peg,' he said.

Peggy moved swiftly around the room. She filled a bowl with warm water from a kettle and then sprinkled salt into it before returning to him.

'Hold this,' she ordered before thrusting the bowl into his hands. Water splashed over the enamel rim into his lap. Jackson watched as she picked some clean cloths and dropped them into the water.

Peggy gently began to wash the bloodstains from his face.

'Thanks, Peg,' Jackson said.

Peggy Smith paused for a moment and looked at him. 'Did Ely's men do this?'

'One of them,' Jackson shrugged. 'He ain't gonna do it to anybody else, though.'

'You killed him?'

'Yep,' Jackson said thoughtfully. 'I killed two

more of them earlier in the Rattler. It seems that I ain't too popular around Broken Lance.'

'Nobody wearing a star ever is in this town,' Peggy noted.

The smiling female continued to clean Jackson's scalp until she had satisfied herself that she had finished with the graze on his head. It had stopped bleeding. Peggy lifted the bowl off his lap and placed it on a table.

'Stand up and take off that shirt, Tim,' she told him. 'I'll get one of my husband's old ones later. It might be a tad snug but this one is ruined.'

'Thank you, Peg,' Jackson said as he rose to his full height and carefully removed the blood-soaked shirt. He dropped it onto the bare boards and felt her hands delicately inspect his ribs. His eyes looked down at the tiny female at his side. Jackson inhaled silently. Her fingers were soft and sent ripples of pleasure through his impressive body.

For a brief moment he forgot about the turmoil he was embroiled in. All thoughts of the gold shipment and the deadly men who destroyed anyone who got in their way evaporated from his mind. All he could think about was the beautiful Peggy Smith standing beside him.

Peggy looked at his hairy chest and briefly smiled.

'I'll have to sew up one of these grazes, Tim,' she said reluctantly. 'It'll keep bleeding otherwise.'

'Do what you like,' he said in a low simmering drawl. 'I'm just grateful you're willing to help me.'

She eased the high-shouldered man back down upon the chair and then felt something long forgotten stir deep within her. It was a feeling which, since the death of her husband, had lain dormant. She glanced up from the wounds and looked at his face. Peggy touched his cheek and drew his eyes to her own.

Emotion smouldered deep within the two.

Neither spoke.

CHAPTER NINETEEN

Darkness had arrived by the time that the side door of the café opened. Coal-tar street lights had replaced the blazing sun and bathed the sprawling settlement of Broken Lance in a different kind of hue. Now a strange, eerie amber illumination lit up the streets, allowing the town's citizens to continue their activities long after the sun had disappeared beyond the rolling hills.

The town had been quiet since the injured sheriff had inexplicably vanished from sight. Only the blacksmith had witnessed where Jackson had gone after his high-shouldered pal had left the livery stable shortly after returning to town.

Only Griff knew why he had taken sanctuary in the café.

Rested and patched up, Jackson stared down at the tiny female and smiled. He went to speak but her fingers had touched his lips before any words could leave his mouth.

Peggy Smith smiled at the towering lawman and then closed and locked her door. Jackson turned and stared out into the main street. It was quiet now and bathed in a million ominous shadows. Shadows which Jackson knew could conceal countless enemies within their depths.

He adjusted his gun-belt and strode along the boardwalk toward the main street. Reaching the corner, Jackson glanced over his shoulder at the café which was now bathed in darkness.

A wry satisfied smile etched his chiselled features as he stepped down onto the sand and walked towards the livery. With each step, Jackson's eyes darted around the quiet street searching every shadow for unseen assassins.

Having already tasted their bullets' fury, Jackson did not want to feel their wrath again, if he could avoid it.

Jackson reached the wide open barn doors of the livery stable and paused for a moment. He looked down the street at the brightest of its many structures. Lights spilled out into the street from the saloon.

'Don't worry about the Rattler, Tim,' Griff said

as he emerged from the dimly lit stable and stood beside the towering figure of the young lawman. 'None of Ely's henchmen have come back to town since they rode out earlier.'

Jackson raised an eyebrow. 'They ain't?'

'Nope, they ain't,' the blacksmith nodded. 'Must be more than four hours now. You seen the galoots before you went over to the café?'

'I seen them OK,' Jackson recalled before turning and entering the livery stable. He stopped beside the forge and warmed his large hands. 'They must know that the gold shipment is being moved tonight.'

Griff had trailed the lawman from the doors.

'But how could they have found out when them gold miners intend moving that gold, son?' he asked. 'Who told them?'

Jackson gritted his teeth and shook his head. 'Beats me but they must have bin told. Somehow they've learned that Collins is heading from the mine for the railhead at midnight. There's no other reason for all them back-shooters to have all left Broken Lance at the same time.'

The blacksmith frowned. 'What you gonna do, son?'

Jackson thought for a time and then glanced at

the face of his troubled friend. There was genuine concern in Griff's face.

'I'm gonna try and stop them, old timer,' he said bluntly.

'I'll saddle your grey.'

Jackson nodded. 'I'm obliged.'

As the blacksmith feverishly readied the grey stallion he looked at the young man with the tin star still defiantly pinned to his chest.

'What about Ely?' the blacksmith asked. 'He's the real trouble in Broken Lance.'

Jackson nodded in agreement. 'I know he is, but his riders will surely kill a lot of Collins' men if I don't try and stop them.'

Griff patted the blanket on the back of the grey horse.

'What you gonna do about Ely, though?' he asked as he placed Jackson's saddle on the tall grey. 'That cruel bastard creates misery just for the fun of it. The womenfolk that work for him look darn pitiful.'

Jackson exhaled. He knew that it was impossible to be in two places at once. 'When I'm finished with his bushwhackers I'll settle with Buren Ely.'

Griff tightened the cinch strap of the saddle and dropped the fender. The big man led the grey to its master.

'No jury would have the guts to find him guilty, Tim,' the blacksmith said as he handed the reins to Jackson and watched the star-packer mount his horse. 'Every man in town is too scared of that critter to put a rope around his neck.'

Jackson looked down at the blacksmith.

'A rope is too good for Ely, Griff.' The sheriff tapped his spurs and allowed the stallion to walk toward the open doors. 'That's why I intend killing him when I get back.'

Griff rested his knuckles on his hips and watched as Jackson rode through the amber light and headed toward the distant hills.

'*If* you get back, son,' he said solemnly.

CHAPTER TWENTY

Jackson had been riding for what felt an eternity atop his magnificent grey stallion. The large overhead moon made the rolling hills appear as though it was the middle of day, and yet the strange eerie light bore no relation to sunshine. The acrid stench of the distant gold smelter drifted on the air as Jackson continued to follow the hoof tracks of the lethal gunman's horses.

The hoof tracks bathed in moonlight made it easy for the star-packer to follow his prey. A driving force told him that he had to prevent them from executing not only Buren Ely's plan but every one of Collins' guards.

Jackson steered the intrepid stallion up a rise at a speed few other horses could have equalled. As he rode, he kept staring down at the hoof tracks in the sand.

The grey reached the top of the grassless hill and its master hauled his long leathers up to his chest. A cloud of whispering dust floated off into the air above a deep chasm.

Jackson steadied the powerful horse.

The tracks led down the steep slope into a place which was masked by blackness. Jackson dismounted and held his mount's bridle to quiet the excited animal as his eyes vainly searched for a glimpse of the men he instinctively knew were down there somewhere.

The shadows seemed to cover half the land below his high vantage point. Jackson bit his lip and knelt as his gloved hand brushed the dry ground.

'They're down there, boy,' he whispered to his horse. 'But *where* are they?'

Jackson rested beside his mount for a few endless minutes when something drew his attention. The star-packer glanced to his left and narrowed his eyes.

His eyes squinted hard over his wide shoulder until they located the source of the unusual sound. Slowly the young sheriff rose back to his full height and stared at the sight which surprised him.

It was the gold wagon.

Jackson removed the glove from his left hand and then poked his fingers into his pocket and removed his watch by its chain. He flicked open the lid of the battered case and stared at the dial.

As he had figured, it was nowhere close to midnight.

'Seven-twenty,' he said, before snapping the lid shut and returning the timepiece to his pants pocket. He rubbed his jaw as his mind raced. 'Zack Collins either lied to me when they were heading for the railhead spur, or something has made him change his plans.'

The grey stallion nodded as though agreeing with its master. Jackson wrapped his reins around his hand, grabbed his saddle horn and then mounted the tall horse.

Jackson had no sooner found his right stirrup with his boot when he saw the distant smoke snaking up into the sky in the opposite direction. The sheriff stood in his stirrups and stared at the smoke. Eventually he realized what it was that he was looking at. It was the train at the railhead. '

The locomotive was waiting for its precious cargo.

He cast his eyes back at the steep slope. It was churned up by the gunmen's horses' hoofs as they had descended down into the blackness.

Although the tracks led down the slope to where the heavily escorted wagon was also heading, Jackson realized that it would be foolishness for him to ride blindly into a possible trap.

Jackson turned the stallion.

With the expertise only someone raised as a cowboy could manage, the star-packer guided the stallion along the perilous incline and then thundered down the loose surface of the slope.

Fearlessly, Jackson descended the dangerous hillside at pace. Soon he escaped the glaring moonlight and rode deeper into the shadows. Although he could not see where the gunmen might be hiding, he knew they could not see him either.

Jackson reached the level ground and stopped his mount.

He swung the horse full circle in a vain attempt to spot the men he sought. There was still no sign of them. Jackson steadied the grey and dismounted.

No matter how hard he tried Jackson could not find any hoof tracks on the sand. Then the rumbling noise from the distant wagon filled his ears again.

Jackson threw his aching body up on to the back of the grey and watched as the wagon drew closer. It was flanked by half a dozen outriders. The moonlight danced off their Winchester barrels.

Jackson gathered up his long leathers and started towards the approaching vehicle when all Hell broke loose.

Without warning, the distant darkness exploded into action as hot lead flashed like lightning strikes. Jackson watched as rods of lethal lead spewed their deafening venom from both sides of the approaching wagon. Bullets tore the guards from their horses. Jackson gasped in horror as the sound of gunshots rang out along the valley.

Jackson knew that he was not watching a gunfight. He was watching a slaughter.

With no thought for his own safety, Jackson dragged his rifle from its scabbard, cranked its mechanism and spurred. He drove the grey on towards the blinding flashes of merciless bullets at breakneck speed.

The very thing he had come to try and prevent was already happening before his eyes. None of Ely's men heard the approaching horse as they unleashed their fury at the gold wagon's guards.

Like crazed men drunk on their own success, the gunmen blasted at the outriders until they had all fallen into the dust as the armoured wagon forged on.

Jackson could see the bushwhackers firing at the wagon but their bullets bounced off the metal plates like firecrackers.

It was like attacking a buffalo with toothpicks.

The wagon's horses and its driver were well protected from the gunmen's bullets. The armoured wagon continued along the trail toward the grey stallion as Jackson guided the animal out of its path and then hauled rein.

The vehicle thundered passed him as Jackson watched the bushwhackers rush to their mounts and start their pursuit. The lawman could see about six horsemen riding straight toward him as they pursued the heavily laden wagon.

Jackson knew that the riders were determined to prevent it from reaching the relative safety of the distant locomotive and the railroad spur.

He was the only thing standing between them and the gold.

Jackson fired his rifle at the riders until its magazine was empty. A symphony of deafening white flashes erupted from their guns and cut a trail toward him and his trusty grey.

Jackson thrust his rifle back into its scabbard and drew one of his six-shooters. He cocked and fired as he swung the grey around. He saw one of the gunmen knocked off his saddle by the impact of his bullet. There was no time to see if any of his other shots had found their targets.

He spurred and chased the fleeing vehicle.

Jackson ate dust as he closed the distance between the wagon and his powerful stallion. More shots whizzed by the lawman.

Within minutes his grey stallion had caught up with the wagon. Jackson knew that even with eight horses pulling the metal-clad vehicle, it was far too heavy for its team of valiant horses to maintain its pace.

Jackson had a choice to make.

It was the most important and dangerous of his entire life. He rode alongside the body of the wagon and then leapt from his saddle. Jackson's hands grabbed the top of the riveted roof as his legs dangled precariously over the large rear wheel. Mustering every scrap of his strength Jackson clambered up the metal side. He dragged himself over the side of the wagon and lay flat on its roof.

Jackson looked at his grey as the intrepid animal continued to keep pace with the labouring vehicle. He screwed up his eyes and looked at the clouds of dust the wagon was kicking up. Then he saw the riders as they started firing again.

He drew both his guns and Jackson started to fire at the wagon's pursuers as they shot at him. Bullets ricocheted off the iron plates and showered him in sparks. The star-packer continued to squeeze his triggers at the gunmen.

One by one he picked them off from the high rooftop of the wagon. As the last of them went cartwheeling over his saddle cantle and crashed into the dust behind his horse's hoofs, Jackson slowly got on to his knees and then stood.

As the wagon filled with golden bricks entered the rail yard and rolled up next to the awaiting locomotive and crane Jackson whistled to his horse.

The grey rode closer to the slowing vehicle as its master leapt from the wagon's rooftop onto his saddle. Jackson grabbed his reins, swung the horse around and then spurred away from the railhead.

Zack Collins emerged from the fortified wagon and caught sight of the young star-packer as he thundered out of the railhead and headed back toward Broken Lance.

'Where in tarnation is *he* going in such a hurry?' he wondered.

FINALE

Broken Lance was quiet as the lone horseman rode into its main street and slowed the pace of the grey stallion as he approached the Rattler saloon. A few drunken men staggered along the boardwalk as Jackson eased back on his reins and dismounted the tall horse. He looped his reins over the hitching rail and then secured them.

Jackson eyed the saloon like a hungry puma watching its chosen prey. The saloon, like the rest of the town, was now quieter than it had been earlier that day. Yet its lantern light still cascaded out on to the street and stretched across its sand.

There was little noise coming from the heart of the saloon apart from the sound of a few men trying to sing along to an out of tune piano.

The high-shouldered lawman leaned back and cast his attention to the balcony above the porch overhang. Every window was lit up.

Before Jackson stepped up on to the saloon boardwalk he caught sight of a familiar figure hastily approaching him. It was Jefferson Healy, looking far more nervous than Jackson had ever seen him before. The mayor stepped into the amber lantern light and grabbed Jackson's arm.

'Where you been?' he asked anxiously.

'I just made sure that your gold wagon got safely to the railhead, Mr Mayor,' Jackson sighed. 'How come you look so troubled?'

Healy leaned close to the tall man.

'They found the body of one of my partners up in that alleyway earlier, Tim.' He pointed. 'He stank of laudanum and hard liquor. I reckon they plied him with it to find out when the shipment was being taken from the mine to the train.'

Jackson nodded. 'That must be why Ely's henchmen lit out of here so fast earlier, Mayor. They were waiting in ambush and killed all of the wagon's guards.'

Healy went pale. 'My God! Where'd Ely's gunmen go?'

'My guess is they all went to Hell,' Jackson said as he checked his six-shooters and eased the mayor aside. 'They're probably there by now.'

Healy gasped. 'You killed them?'

Jackson nodded and stepped up onto the board-walk and looked over the swing doors. His large hands pushed the doors inward and he strode into the saloon. The few men that were still inside the Rattler noticed the grim-faced lawman with the gleaming star pinned to his shirt. They stopped drinking and staggered out of the saloon fast.

The bartender watched as Jackson walked across the sawdust-strewn floor towards him. He gulped.

'You looking for the boss?' he stammered.

Jackson just nodded. 'His men tried to kill me over in the valley so I intend making him pay.'

'What happened to the boys?' Lever asked.

'I already made them pay,' Jackson said. 'Where's Ely?'

'You lookin' for me, star-packer?' Buren Ely shouted from the top of the staircase. 'Well, here I am.'

Jackson eyed the rancid saloon keeper and stepped away from the horseshoe bar and its counter.

'I surely am, Ely,' he nodded. 'I'm kinda sick of your boys trying to kill me. By my reckoning the only way to stop a snake from sinking its fangs into you is to cut its head off.'

'Is that so?' Ely grunted.

Jackson nodded. 'It is.'

Ely grinned and then swiftly pulled a shotgun from behind his back. He aimed it down at the lawman. 'When my boys get here they'll cut you into little bits, Sheriff.'

'They're all dead, Ely,' Jackson informed. 'They got themselves killed trying to hold up the gold miners' wagon down yonder.'

A rage swept over the saloon keeper with the realization that his plans had been ruined. Unable to contain his venomous fury his thumbs hauled back on the shotgun's hammer.

'You'll pay for that, you stinking lawman!' Ely yelled out as he pulled on the trigger.

Jackson ducked, turned a table over and felt the impact of the buckshot as it ripped into the green baize. He rose back to his full height as Ely expelled the smoking cartridges from his shotgun and prepared to reload.

'I'd not do that if I was you,' he warned as he drew one of his guns and eased its hammer back. 'You'll surely die if you do.'

'You ain't me,' Buren Ely snapped and levelled the shotgun at the sheriff again.

Jackson fired. The lethally accurate bullet hit the saloon keeper dead centre. The lawman watched Ely drop the weapon as blood spread over his shirt. Within seconds the depraved owner of the Rattler was covered in his own gore. He toppled forward like a felled tree and crashed down the staircase, finally coming to a halt at Jackson's boots. The lifeless eyes stared blankly up at the young lawman. Jackson silently turned, holstered his smoking six-shooter and walked back out of the saloon. He paused beside the town mayor.

'Is it over, Tim?' Healy asked the towering lawman.

'It's over, Mr Mayor.' Jackson pulled his long leathers free of the hitching rail and walked down the lantern-lit street toward the livery. As he reached the stable Griff was there to greet him and take the reins of the grey.

'You OK, son?' he asked as the door of the café opened and the handsome female emerged. When Peggy saw Jackson she beamed.

Jackson grinned. 'I'm fine, Griff. Mighty fine.'

The blacksmith watched the high-shouldered sheriff stride up to the female and wrap his powerful arms around her. They went into the café and closed the door behind them.

Griff raised his eyebrows. 'I sure hope he remembers to take his spurs off.'